When the starship *Elysian Dawn* crash-landed on a strange planet eighteen years into its journey, a joint rescue mission was launched by Terra and Shiva. The rescue failed, and everyone involved had to pick up the pieces . . . and find new dreams.

New Dreams
Copyright © 2018 Sally Odgers
ISBN: 978-1-4874-2157-1
Cover art by Martine Jardin

Published by eXtasy Books Inc or
Devine Destinies, an imprint of eXtasy Books Inc

Look for us online at:
www.eXtasybooks.com or www.devinedestinies.com

New Dreams
Elydian Dawn Book 3

By

Sally Odgers

DEDICATION

For everyone who has had to find new dreams

AUTHOR NOTES

This Elydian saga began back in November 1999 during a writers' residency in a cottage at a university. For three weeks, I slept during the day and worked feverishly at night when the computer in the writers' cottage was free, tumbling into bed about six o'clock in the morning. I gave workshops, went for walks, shivered in unseasonably cold weather and swept innumerable millipedes off the walls. I averaged around 10,000 words a session. It was wonderful, but during the last few days my hands started to swell and ache, and within a couple of weeks of getting home, I'd succumbed to chronic tendonitis in both hands, a condition that continues to plague me eighteen years later. I'd written two full novels and part of another, but I had to put them aside. In 2016, I realised the backstory wanted to be told. Okay, I could do 30,000 words, and if it worked out, I might finally finish my series. 113,000 words later, I had a book. This was too long, so after consideration and discussion with my invaluable editor, I made it into three books. These are *Elysian Dawn*, *The Silvering* and *New Dreams*.

THE STORY SO FAR

In the twenty-third century, a new propulsion system was invented. For the first time, the idea of settling planets outside our solar system was feasible. The Western Alliance, comprising western countries from the 21st Century, began work on the ambitious *Elysian Dawn* project with the idea of sending a thousand hand-picked humans out to Magellan Sixteen. Even with the new Faster-than-Light drive—FetTL—his journey would take many generations. The company in charge of selecting the people and providing the ship was Outward-Bound.

In 2254, three ships were poised for departure, with more crowding behind them. *Elysian Dawn* was the biggest and oldest, using a Mark One FetTL drive. *Ganges*, owned by the Eastern Alliance and bound for the planet Shiva, was next, using a Mark Two FetTL drive. In close third place was *Zulu Queen*, from the African-Greek-Italian Alliance and bound for the planet Juno. The race was on for *First Launch*.

Eighteen years later, due to the high-speed FetTL engines of *Ganges* and *Zulu Queen*, settlements were flourishing on Shiva and Juno. The Shivans ran an ambitious modified communist system, grooming elite young Citizens to take over from the Terran Regents known as Provosts. Shivan Citizens were forbidden to leave their planet of birth. Peaceful and courteous High Ladies ran Juno. They forbade the importation of plants and animals.

Elysian Dawn, with the slower engine and most ambitious destination, was eighteen years into her multigenerational

1

journey when she crashed on the single satellite of the Caspar system. The people aboard believed they were eighteen years from any hope of rescue, but they were wrong. The newly-developed FetTL Mark Three ship, *Indira*, could be with them in days. Outward-Bound on Terra and Krishna Tower on Shiva made a deal to rescue the survivors.

By the time *Indira* arrived in orbit around the newly named planet of Elydia, further disaster had overtaken the survivors of *Elysian Dawn*. A condition called the racking had attacked the colonists, killing all the adults. The younger children were unaffected, but many older teenagers also died. The oldest survivors included Marianne Arcadia, who was seventeen, Finn Causeway, sixteen, and Edsen Balm, fifteen.

It was agreed the youngest orphans would be taken aboard *Indira* first and repatriated to Shiva. Finn Causeway, his brother, Farne, and another older survivor called Claire Atlantis volunteered to go as well.

Indira set off for Shiva, but a second round of the racking killed Finn, Farne, and Claire. For the first time, younger children died as well. So did Ambassador Jameel Singh, who had landed on the planet without an iso-suit. Horrified, the medics aboard *Indira* decreed the ship must return the remaining rescued children to Elydia, and all personnel must go into quarantine.

CHAPTER ONE: RETURN TO SENDER

Indira in space– Shivan Year 6 Day 579-80
Doctor Daffodil Lan

"Everybody loves a rescue, so long as it's successful." Doctor Harry Fejoa's voice was dry.

Daffodil Lan didn't want to admit it, but she knew Harry was right. The crew and passengers of the interplanetary ferryship *Indira* had made the rescue attempt from all sorts of motives. She had come along partly to add some practical experience to her resume. That wasn't noble, but she was a junior doctor with her way to make in the world. She *had* wanted to save the orphans of the crashed colony ship *Elysian Dawn*. She'd pictured it time after time.

The reality of a hundred traumatised children to care for crashed in on her rosy imaginings. And that was *before* they started to die. The senior doctors decreed the remaining children must be restored to the planet they were calling Elydia. Furthermore, there was a real risk of carrying the contamination or infection or whatever it was on the rescue ship.

They could not afford to carry the deadly racking back to Shiva and Terra, so there was just one thing to do.

The medical lockdown of Shiva's new state-of-the-art ferryship wasn't something to be undertaken lightly.

The captain had to be persuaded, the Provosts on board briefed, Outward-Bound, former owners of the crashed ship, notified, and Krishna Tower, which had organised the rescue, informed. It was a mess, Daffodil knew, and a mess that had come from the best of intentions.

Dorotea Suchet, the senior paediatrician, made methodical suggestions. "We'll have to let Citizen Singh at Krishna Tower know. Where's Ambassador Singh? Has anyone briefed him? He might want to talk to his sister."

"I couldn't find him." Daffodil found she was practically wringing her hands.

"You've looked already?"

"Yes, before—before all this started. Amrita wanted him, and I thought she should go to him. After all, he's planning to adopt her." She explained how she'd failed to find the ambassador.

Dorotea nodded, her usually cheerful face falling into lines so for once, she looked her age. "It sounds as if you made a methodical job of the search, Daff."

"You want me to look again?"

"No. We don't have time to go running all over the ship, retracing what you did already. Get that communications tech—Dov Talman—to put a call for him. He hasn't taken the lander again?"

"I checked that. But why would he? We've left the planetary orbit so there's nowhere he could go."

"So, he's still on board. We need him, and we also need to get these children segregated. It may be too late, but we'll get the older ones into isolation. It may minimise trauma to the young ones if this thing progresses. Doctor Benz will do the autopsies with Doctor Fejoa and look for any clue as to what causes the condition. Daffodil, you've seen three cases now. In your judgement, is it a disease or a condition? How is it communicated, or does it develop in isolation? What are the first symptoms? How do they progress?"

Daffodil was rattled, but these calm questions took her back to her not-so-distant student days. She took a deep breath and gave her opinion.

"It looks like a condition to me, and there must be invisible early symptoms. Before it began, I noticed both Claire Atlantis and Finn Causeway had isolated themselves and were sitting alone. That was normal for Claire, but not for Finn. Claire seemed disconnected. Disorientated. She asked questions she would have asked when we first landed on the planet. Come to think of it, Farne did that, too." Farne Causeway was Finn's younger brother. He had been the third rescued child to die.

"What was happening from their perspective?" Dorotea asked, still calmly.

Daffodil shrugged. "I don't know. They were too withdrawn to reach. I did try talking to Claire and Farne. It was too late for Finn. He died before I realised anything was wrong."

"What happened with Claire? Did she become unresponsive?"

"She started to exhibit the typical signs of a tonic-clonic seizure. I administered lax-a-pen two-cc, but she went into full seizure and died quickly."

"Did you use lax-a-pen on the other two?"

"Not on Finn, because he was dead already. I used it on Farne, and then, after the first seizure, Doctor Benz suggested we double the dose. We did so, but it had no effect. The seizures progressed, and he died during the third."

"The younger boy had a more protracted bout, then," Dorotea said.

"I suppose so, though I didn't see Finn's bout. I assume it was quick. Farne survived longer than Claire."

"We know what to look out for then, older children isolating themselves and losing focus."

Daffodil snapped, "Knowing that doesn't help if we can't treat it! And what about the younger children? Some of them seem unusually disengaged."

Dorotea made a calming motion with her hand. "We'll see what the autopsies show. If necessary, we'll put the remaining at-risk children into stasus until we reach the planet."

Daffodil eyed her senior colleague unhappily. "What use is taking them back to the planet? We know a lot of the Terra-born died there of this condition. If the second wave has already hit, the remaining ship-born could be dead already. Abandoning children to die on a deserted planet is a violation of our oath and our duty."

"Do no harm," Dorotea said softly.

"Exactly!"

"It's a noble sentiment, but sometimes harm is unavoidable. If it comes down to harm to a few hundred ship-born and probably *Indira*'s payload, against harm coming to Shiva or Terra if this thing gets loose, then our duty lies in doing the least harm."

"I suppose so," Daffodil muttered. She wished fruitlessly to be anywhere but there.

Doctor Dorotea Suchet

Leaving young Doctor Lan to digest her comments, Dorotea sent one of the techs to have Ambassador Singh hailed. Following that, he was to contact the ship-born remaining on the planet.

The call went out for Jameel Singh, but although it echoed through *Indira*, there was no response.

When appealed to, Dov Talman, the chief communications tech, admitted he could do an override and track the young ambassador's whereabouts, but he pointed out that was unethical and could get him sacked.

Sharply told that not doing it could contribute to a great many deaths, including his, he agreed to track down Ambassador Singh.

"He's in Passim Dee's room . . . the mineralogist's quarters," he reported after a brief scan of the ship.

The door was locked, but the captain used the emergency override.

Dorotea almost groaned aloud as she realised Ambassador Jameel Singh was dead. At first, it looked as if his demise was due to misadventure, a fall that fractured his skull. A brief examination proved the fall and fracture had merely hastened his death, and that may have been merciful. His body showed the same seizure damage as the three dead ship-born.

The discovery had dire auspices. Not only was Citizen Meera Singh's personal liaison and brother dead, but he was the first case among the Terrans and Terra-born on *Indira*.

Dorotea Suchet didn't have the luxury of personal panic. She had to work with the other medics to minimise the damage.

"Commtech Talman!" She made her voice as authoritative as she could. "Are you able to use Ambassador Singh's comm-set to contact the ship-born on the planet?"

He nodded, looking rattled. He wasn't the only one.

"The designated user down there is Edsen Balm. We need information from him, and we need the right questions asked in the right order."

He nodded again.

"Right. First, ascertain he is still alive and healthy. If not, speak with anyone you can raise on the com. Understand?"

"Yes. Speak with Edsen Balm if possible."

"Good. Next, ask if there has been a recurrence of the racking among those left on the surface. Has anyone who recovered from the first bout had a resurgence of symptoms? If so, was it fatal?

"Next, ask if there are any new cases among the younger

ship-born who weren't badly affected or maybe weren't affected at all, the first time around.

"If the answer is no, ask if he, or anyone else, can remember exactly what Ambassador Singh did when he landed on
the planet. We need to reconstruct his experience. It can't be
a coincidence that he is the only one of the landing party to
die."

So far. She didn't voice that aloud.

She gave Talman a few seconds to absorb the information
and then had him relay it back. "Are you ready?"

"Yes."

She watched as he put the call through to the planet, not
because she wanted to intimidate the commtech, but because
she wanted the information immediately and first-hand.

To her considerable relief, Edsen Balm answered the call,
looking much as he had when she last saw him on the planet's surface, a floppy-haired and pugnacious boy in his mid-
dle teens. His posture was less defeated, and his eyes looked
brighter and more focused, so it seemed all was well among
the orphans left on the planet.

CHAPTER TWO: OPERATION NOAH

Planet surface– Shiptime 18 8 10 – 11
Edsen Balm

Edsen answered the comm-set when it flashed. "Jameel? Have you found out any more about the possible predator?"

A face came into focus on the screen and flickered out, but Edsen had seen enough to know it wasn't Jameel Singh. This was a person he didn't know.

He tried again. "Edsen Balm, comm-set *Keeper*." That was the title Marianne had suggested he should use.

The screen flickered again, showing the serious visage of a man with light-reddish hair. His mother, Carolina's hair had been that colour, but now she lay buried in the soil next to the crashed ship. Edsen winced at the thought.

"Commtech Dov Talman," the man introduced himself. After the lag, his voice continued, "Are you people all still well?"

That was an odd way to put it. Edsen looked about. Marianne, the three Moon blossoms, Zeb, and Granton were discussing the animal tanks. The Elves, as they'd started calling the older children of eleven and twelve, were setting up some of the prefabricated shelters unloaded from *Elysian Dawn* during Hanaka Moon's brief mobilisation of the Terraborn.

Moon was dead now, but she had given them a valuable example before falling to the racking, and her daughters

Momo, Sakura, and Panji were carrying on from her example.

"What's left of us are all well, and we're busy," he said, frowning. He wanted to speak with Jameel or Finn Causeway. "Are you on your way to—" He broke off. *Dead air.* Hadn't Jameel said these things didn't fail?

He touched the screen, and the light came back on.

The worried face looked back at him, lips moving.

"Say again?"

"Are you okay?"

"Yes," Edsen said emphatically. The ones who'd chosen to stay had decided they would show no sign of uncertainty to any of the Terrans. And it wasn't a lie. Now so many of the smallest children were safely on *Indira* life was easier. Most of the remaining toddlers had family on the planet. *Someone to love them,* as Momo Moon put it in her serious way. She said that was important. No one could thrive without someone to love them. They'd grow all wrong.

Edsen had started to realise a year or so ago that love came in different guises. He gathered Momo meant the one where someone thought you were nice and liked to be with you, and might come and hug you, just because.

Marianne waved her hand to get his attention and gave a wide smile.

The smile wasn't for him, worse luck. It was just a hint of what she wanted him to show the commtech. Edsen managed to achieve a smile of his own. It felt weird, and he realised he never had smiled much. His parents Carolina and Eduard had been serious people, and he'd learned by example.

"Can I talk to Jameel? Or Finn?" he asked.

The lips moved. Edsen realised Talman was saying *Say again,* and he repeated his request before the sound came through.

The resulting garble meant neither of them heard the other.

"Jameel," Edsen said, exaggerating his lip movement.

"Ambass –" The word broke.

Edsen shook his head in frustration. He must be going wrong, somehow. The screen went blank, flared, and flickered. Regretfully, Edsen turned it off.

"What's wrong?" Marianne came to stand beside him.

"I don't know. This comm-set isn't working. I must be doing something wrong."

"More likely it's the comm-set going wrong, not you. Even the Terra-tat went wrong after the crash."

"After eighteen years!"

"It's not your fault, Ed. You're doing your best, and it's a good best." She put a hand on his shoulder and squeezed gently.

He knew she meant what she said. Marianne always did.

"Thanks. I'll ask Jameel how to fix it next time I talk to him."

"Never mind that now. We're waiting for your vote about the animals. We can't wait any longer to decide what to do."

Edsen drew a big breath. He didn't know how to handle animals. None of them did. There had been so much death, though that he couldn't face letting living things die without giving them a chance. "Let's get them out here in the wind," he said.

He knew from Marianne's joyful face he'd said the right thing.

None of them wanted to enter *Elysian Dawn,* but at least the stores and animal tanks were not near the family level. Edsen had been in several times with the sympathetic techs from *Indira,* and now the bodies of the lost ones located outside the family level were laid out neatly, shrouded in what the techs called *stasi-sheet*. He'd decided to wait for a while before they continued with the burials.

He led the small group of six Noahs, as Marianne termed them, to the hold. The candles flickered, but by now more cracks had developed in *Elysian Dawn,* and the bright glare of the star Caspar illuminated some of the tanks.

"Are they alive?" Marianne asked.

"This one's heart is still beating," Momo said, after staring fixedly at it for thirty seconds.

Now that they were standing at the tanks, the release seemed less of a good idea.

The tanks were mounted on gyros, so at least they were the right way up.

"What do they eat?" Granton Farsee, a stocky, fair-haired boy, asked.

"Grass, I think. There's one story about horses eating humans because a king wanted people to be scared, but that wasn't a true story." Marianne sounded certain, which was a good thing.

"I hope not. Don't want to be eaten by a horse," Granton said.

"Let's start with a sheep," Edsen suggested. After all, it was smaller.

The mechanical levers that opened the tanks were almost too stiff to turn, but they managed. The brown goop that sustained the sheep drained through a grill in the bottom of the tank. Edsen hoped it wasn't flooding the remaining stores since the floor wasn't where it should be. There were eight sheep in that tank, all covered in closely-packed curly hair. As the thick liquid drained out, their hoofs touched the floor of the tank, and they collapsed in a messy heap.

"Are they dead?"

No one wanted to touch them. This was the first time they'd ever seen an animal clearly, and they weren't impressed.

Then Momo said, "When babies are born they look like this. When they're cleaned up, they look more like people."

As she spoke, the sheep showed signs of life, kicking, heaving and uttering strange cries.

"How do we get them out of the ship?" Granton asked.

Marianne answered, "I think we'll have to let them find their own way. Maybe they'll follow us. I've read about sheep following their shepherd. That's what the person who looks after sheep is called."

No one else had a better idea, so Edsen started back along the way to the exit. To his relief, the sheep tottered after him, still making their plaintive calls. Once they were outside, they stood looking around while the Elves and younger children working nearby flocked to see. Then one of the sheep made an odd leap. The surrounding children laughed, and some of the smaller ones jumped back, so suddenly they fell over.

Soon all the sheep were making their odd jumps, and then one dropped its head to the silvery grass and bit some off. The look on its face was ludicrous, but it chewed, and bit some more.

"See? They eat grass." Marianne sounded triumphant.

"I hope they don't get the racking," Sherry Cliffside said.

That sobered them all.

"We should wait and see if this lot's all right before we bring the others out."

"Yes, but if we wait a few days, the ones in the tanks will be dead anyway."

Marianne turned to Edsen. "What did Jameel say about the animals he saw? When did he see them?"

"I think he saw them on a comm-set. You remember the other man who came on the lander? That first time?"

She said, "Passim Dee."

13

"I think *he* saw them, and Jameel told us. It was a day or so *that* way." He pointed.

"We'll go and see when we get the shelters finished."

"And I want to try planting some of the seedstock from the daily stores, so we can have some normal food," Sherry said.

"Are there any books with sheep in them?"

The excited babble broke out again, and then Marianne clapped her hands. "I think we need to get the other animals out and let them have a chance. They're going to die if we don't. They only *might* die if we do. And if we're going to do it, we have to do it now."

This time, the trek to the store hold was more optimistic. Edsen eyed the horses with a little trepidation, but Marianne seemed determined they should be freed from the tanks, and so they were.

More goop drained out, and the looming creatures crumpled to the floor as the sheep had done. As they took their first breaths in nineteen years, they stopped looking like shapeless hulks and became living beings. They seemed frightened, and an attempt to move them out as they had the sheep led to Sherry being pushed violently against the floor that had once been the wall.

Granton and Sakura checked her over, and fortunately, she was dazed rather than damaged, but they decided to be more careful after that.

"Better warn the Elves to keep the little kids away from them. We don't want them getting squashed," Sherry said as she recovered.

"You'll do that?" Marianne asked, and the girl said she would.

"I think we should try to make another opening, so they can go out straight away instead of having to go along the way we came in." Edsen indicated one of the bigger cracks in the ship's skin and pulled experimentally at it. Some of it came away, but the job was going to take too long. Granton came to help, but then Zeb indicated a recessed handle grip behind the tanks.

"What's that?"

The other two came to see and tugged experimentally. It moved, first sluggishly, and then in a rush.

Edsen peered through the gap they'd made, and spotted two recessed wheels, similar to those that had guarded the door to the long-term store. "I think this is the way they were meant to go out," he opined.

The rest of the Noahs came to see.

"It makes sense to have a way out close by," Marianne said.

"I suppose the animal *Keepers* knew," Momo said wistfully.

It seemed she felt the loss of knowledge as badly as he did.

By the time Sherry returned from warning the children to keep clear of the animals, they'd managed to half-open the hatch. It was at an odd angle, and the folding walkway didn't reach the ground, but Edsen thought if the animals saw an easy exit they would take it.

There were more tanks of sheep, and several of what Marianne said were goats. Hens and ducks came forth in dozens, soggy lumps of cloth-like substance with strange orange and pink feet.

Even with the new exit, it took the best part of that day and night to clear out most of the tanks, and some of the animals were dead. Nevertheless, Edsen was entranced to see crowds of them on the second morning, moving around the ship, eating grass. The ducks had all disappeared, but when the Elves took the small children for their morning wash, they came back indignantly reporting the washing pond was full of ducks.

Some of the other animals had gone right away, but that didn't matter. As Marianne pointed out, using the animals wasn't the point. They knew it was possible to ride a horse, and to use a sheep's wool to make clothing, but as none of them had the faintest notion of how to do it, that would have to wait, perhaps forever. For now, it was about life, and chances, for everyone.

Feeling almost happy, Edsen went back to the tanks with Marianne to release the final few.

As the last batch of ducks departed from the ship, making their strange sounds and no doubt heading to the pond like the others, Marianne stretched her arms above her head, raising her chin.

Light fell across her cheek, and Edsen blinked. The silver colouration they'd all noticed had spread, and Marianne's cheek glowed. In some ways, she looked very unlike the Marianne he used to watch for in the gardens, but in others, she was familiar again.

"What?" she said, smiling at him.

"What?"

"You're staring at me, Ed."

Flid it. She'd noticed. "I was just thinking you look better." He touched the bruised flesh of her injured wrist, which was no longer so discoloured. Without premeditation, he said, "You're not dead inside anymore, are you?"

He thought she might snap at him, but instead, she shrugged and pushed his hair back from his eyes as if he were Aleph or Bede. "You're right. I wouldn't say I feel the way I used to. Maybe I never will again. But you *are* right. It's better. We're going to be okay, I think."

"We are," he said. Because if she was all right again, then so was he.

Marianne changed the subject. "Ed, there were two com-tat families, and lots more that knew about making clothes and things. Do you know if Eduard and Carolina and the Colliers had anything written down?"

"How do you mean?"

"Moon had lots of things written down. I know she had a set of books where she put things like accidents people had, and how to wrap bandages for that kind of injury. Momo has some of them now. Anya was a gardener, and she had lists of plants with drawings. So, did the com-tats have anything?"

"There are some copies of the Celestial charts, I think."

"Where are they?"

He thought back. "They must be still with the Terra-tat. They were stored there because the Colliers made some, and so did Eduard and Carolina. Eduard told me they weren't supposed to, but they did."

"Then do you think there might be something about the animals? We don't know who the *Keepers* and *Heirs* were, and they must all be dead, but if there was more than one family, they might have stored books or papers somewhere they could all get to them when they were needed. There was nothing they had to do except monitor the tanks, so they wouldn't need the books in their rooms."

That sounded sensible to Edsen, but without knowing who the *Keepers* had been . . . then he had an idea. Wouldn't it make sense to keep any documents near the tanks? Not in them, obviously, but somewhere nearby, for when they were needed? He pointed this out to Marianne, and they looked about with surmise.

"There's nowhere they could be here. It's just tanks and walls and floor," Marianne said. She poked about in the hatchway, but there were no storage spaces.

"What about the store hold? That's close."

They went to look, and Edsen felt the usual wave of despair at the boxes, crates, barrels and shelves, all split and spilling their contents. There was so much, and it was all over the place.

"There are books there," Marianne indicated. She picked one up and straightened the crumpled pages. *"Boats and Ships."*

"What are those?" Edsen was confident she'd know, and she did.

"Ships are things people built to use when they cross the water. Do you remember the story about Helen and Paris?"

"The one where Paris wanted Helen even though she was married to someone?" he said uneasily. He *did* remember that story because it had struck a painful chord. Marianne used to belong with Jeremiah. He had liked Jeremiah, and he was sad that he was dead. He loved Marianne, but if he could bring back Jeremiah for her, he would do it.

He sighed, and he realised Marianne was still talking.

"Remember, they had ships? They had to go over the sea to get to Troy. I expect they work the way woolwood moves on the pond when the wind blows it. Remember how we used to float bits of stem down the stream in the gardens?"

Edsen tried to imagine enough water to need ships. The washing pool was big enough for him. "Are there pictures?"

Marianne turned some pages, and gave a jolt of excitement, just as she used to, back when she was happy. "Look! This shows us how to make them."

Edsen pored over the pictures.

"If this book shows us about building ships if we need them, there might be other books showing us things. Maybe the animal books really are here. I know they're not in the daily stores' shelves . . . those are all stories. We'll have to get the Elves to help. They can read the names on the books and sort out the ones that might be useful."

They might have spent a lot more time looking for relevant books, and stacking aside those that seemed useful, but at that point, Marianne's brother Bede came in with Franz Rain on his back. The little boy waved happily to Marianne and Edsen, but Bede looked serious.

"What is it?" Marianne turned from the books immediately.

"The shuttle thing's coming back, Mim."

"What? It can't be. It's supposed to take days to get to Shiva."

"Come and see," Bede urged, so they abandoned the books and headed back into the open air, taking the quicker route through the animal hatch.

CHAPTER THREE: AUTOPSY

Indira in space– Shivan Year 6 Day 580
Doctor Daffodil Lan

Indira would soon be back in orbit around the Caspar satellite. This time there was no hopeful anticipation of a wonderful rescue. Instead, Daffodil felt a sense of creeping horror. *Indira* was a plague ship. She would be equally unwelcome on Terra, Shiva or Juno.

After Jameel Singh's death, she'd hoped the racking was over, but Doctor Suchet reminded her the younger Causeway boy's death was a warning. The second wave of racking was not following the same path as the first.

"It would help if we had a clear picture of the first wave," Dorotea Suchet said. She was clearly frustrated that, for all her careful prompting and Commtech Talman's willingness, they hadn't been able to get clear answers from the shipborn on the planet's surface.

The impression was that all was well. Edsen Balm had said so, more than once, but further communication had broken down to no more than a few syllables.

Talman couldn't understand it. *Indira's* comms were working as usual. He opined it was the comm-set on the surface causing the problem. "The Balm boy must be doing something wrong."

"Aren't they meant to be intuitive interfaces?"

Daffodil was surprised at the snap in the paediatrician's voice.

"The boy should be able to use it easily, but there's no knowing what Ambassador Singh might have forgotten to tell him about it."

Blaming a fifteen-year-old with no formal training or a dead ambassador wasn't helpful, and Daffodil sensed Dorotea's frustration.

Further attempts to contact the surface failed, so the only options were to revert to the original plan of dropping a comm-set to the ship-born, or else to deliver one by lander, as Jameel Singh had done.

And he was dead.

"He chose not to wear an iso-suit. We were on the surface, and we're not affected," Dorotea reminded her.

But Daffodil knew they probably were. They'd dispensed with the iso-suits when they came back onboard. She was afraid. She also felt a sense of defeat. After all this, they were going to deliver the remaining children back to the planet and abandon them there.

The orbit was matched, and *Indira* trembled. Just gravity, as the captain said.

"What's going to happen when we've restored the children to the surface?" Daffodil asked.

"We'll hope and possibly pray they survive," Dorotea said.

"To us. To the ship."

"I don't know. That will be up to the captain in part, and to the governments of Shiva and Terra. At the very least we'll have to stay in space long enough to ensure we're not carrying the condition back to Shiva. Even so, I doubt we'll get clearance to land."

Daffodil was aghast. "We can't just keep moving in space like the *Flying Dutchman!*"

"Not forever, no. It's not practicable. This is a ferryship. It's provisioned for a few weeks, and of course we're not carrying anything like the usual manifest, but we will run out of food," Dorotea agreed.

"And then what?"

"We might find a habitable planet where we can live. Possibly one of the outer spiral worlds. More likely, we'll die in space."

"Starving to death isn't —" Daffodil broke off.

"It won't come to that, Daff. There are more pleasant ways to go. As medics, we have them ready in our pouches."

Daffodil wasn't comforted. She was twenty-five. Volunteering for this rescue mission had seemed a noble thing, an interesting thing and also a good thing for her prospects. Now her name would go down in medical annals for the wrong reasons.

The lander was being prepped for a reconnaissance, designed to deliver a new comm-set to the ship-born. When communication was restored, they'd know what was happening on the surface.

"Who's delivering the comm-set?" Daffodil asked.

"I think it had better be me."

"Can you pilot that lander?"

"Provost Rose is taking me."

Daffodil gazed at her. Shivan Provosts didn't pilot landers. They didn't do anything but make pronouncements and observe events. Before she could comment, a call came from Doctor Benz, requesting the presence of all medical personnel.

"Better suit up," Dorotea said.

Clad in iso-suits, the two entered the room where Doctor Benz, assisted by Harry Fejoa, had performed autopsies on two of the victims.

Gerd Benz nodded an acknowledgement to them. "We chose the female adolescent and the younger male."

"Claire and Farne," Daffodil whispered.

"Why not the ambassador? Surely he's the wild card?" Dorotea said.

"He's also the ambassador, a close family member of a Shivan Citizen. Protocol must be observed," Harry Fejoa said wryly.

"I hardly think protocol is going to matter to us." Dorotea's voice was cool.

Benz glanced at his scrolling notes and slipped into lecture mode.

"We chose these two subjects for a number of reasons. First, their bouts with the seizure disorder were observed, and their deaths monitored. Both were treated unsuccessfully with lax-a-pen, which is the most effective treatment for seizures. The variables were as follows.

"Subject one. Female adolescent Caucasian, estimated fifteen standard years. Apparently normal except for what appeared a superficial discolouration of the epidermis and iris. Had recently undergone a bout of the seizure disorder and recovered without lasting damage. Died after a single tonic-clonic seizure. Observed in a depressed and confused state immediately prior to attack."

Daffodil crossed her arms in front of her. As a surgeon, Benz generally dealt with unconscious patients. Maybe that was why he was able to objectify them. Daffodil hadn't especially liked Claire Atlantis, who was sullen and unhelpful, but she wouldn't have wished the girl's death on anyone.

Benz continued without emotion. "Subject two. Unrelated male pre-adolescent Caucasian, estimated ten to twelve standard years. Apparently normal except for what appeared a superficial discolouration of the epidermis and iris. Had not undergone the disorder previously. Survived two tonic-clonic seizures but succumbed to the third. Observed to be in a distressed and confused state immediately prior to the attack."

He paused. "Do you have anything to add to these obs?" His masked face turned from Daffodil to Dorotea.

"Farne was distressed because his brother had just died in front of him. The confusion came afterwards," Daffodil said.

Benz indicated acceptance. "We now proceed to subjects three and four, which present more variables.

"Subject three. Male adolescent Caucasian, stated to be sixteen standard years, but appeared physically younger. Late maturity, but still within the normal parameters. Exhibited the same discolouration as subjects one and two. Elder brother of subject two. Observed in a depressed state sometime prior to death. Attack not witnessed by any medic. No lax-a-pen administered. Had previously survived an attack while on the planet. Probably succumbed quickly.

"Subject four. Male adult Asian in his early-to-mid-twenties, long-term resident of Shiva. No observation prior to death. No previous attack of the disorder. No lax-a-pen administered. Unknown number of seizures but death may have been due to misadventure comprising a fractured skull."

Daffodil glanced at the shrouded figures on the tables. "What did you find out from the two autopsies?"

If Benz was annoyed at her attempt to cut to the chase, he didn't show it. He said, "We found far more physical anomaly in the subjects than is evident from a brief visual examination. What we took to be superficial discolouration proved symptomatic of a much more complex condition . . ."

Daffodil's mind shied from the pedantic words, and she turned to Harry Fejoa, who had assisted in the autopsies but who did usually deal with living patients. "Doctor Fejoa . . . care to translate?"

He took her aside with what might have been a sympathetic smile if his face had been visible. "Send you to sleep, wouldn't it?"

Maybe, if it hadn't been so horrible. "So, what did you find out?"

"The silver-grey discolouration isn't just on the surface. We found the stuff had gone pretty much through the whole body. It invades the joints, and it infiltrates the nervous system."

Daffodil found she was wringing her hands, something she'd been prone to as a child. She forced them apart. "Have you any idea where it came from? What it is? Is it a parasite? A pathogen?"

"The short answer is, we don't know what it is, but we're pretty sure it originates from the planet surface. In other words, we doubt if *Elysian Dawn* encountered it in space."

He paused, and she pictured him frowning within the suit.

"What?"

"I suspect it's not meant to work that way."

"What way?"

"You know how parasites generally don't kill their host? It's counterproductive if they do. A successful parasite is one that merrily drains off just as much blood as it needs, causing minimal symptoms. Some even provide a reciprocal benefit, though we think of those as symbiotes. Cleaner Wrasse, for example. Those are fish that accompany —"

Daffodil huffed impatiently to show she got it.

"Sorry. What I meant was, I suspect this . . . infestation, for want of a more appropriate word. Maybe encroachment?"

Daffodil growled.

"Sorry again. I don't believe it's trying to kill the host, or even to do any harm. I think it's a systemic adaptive mechanism."

"I see." Her dislike of scientific jargon didn't mean she couldn't understand it. "So that explains why this thing attacked the Terran colonists and ship-born when they arrived on the planet. It doesn't explain why it killed *all* the Terra-born and only *some* of the ship-born and it *doesn't* explain why it's killing the younger children now!"

"Younger children? These three aren't the full tally?" He sounded disconcerted.

"While you and Doctor Benz have been working in here, we've lost three more ship-born children. Aled Kassia, who was six, and Emilia Ocean and Vanessin Wilg, who were both about eighteen months." Her voice quivered as she pronounced the names.

"Are others showing any symptoms?" Fejoa asked.

"It's hard to say. They're all out of their routine, and we don't know their usual demeanour."

"How about the remaining adolescents and pre-adolescents?"

"There aren't any. We concentrated on rescuing the unrelated babies first."

Fejoa's hooded head moved in a fashion that suggested a silent whistle, or perhaps a reaction to the ironic emphasis she put on the word *rescuing*.

"Does this upset your theory?" Daffodil asked.

"No. It just adds to it. This adaptive substance infiltrates the human system, presumably bringing it into line with the planetary environment. It seems to function best with young subjects."

"You mean children."

"Children. Their bones are still growing. Since it's designed to be present in the system from conception, it aligns better with the very young."

"But—"

"Just a minute. Let me finish this thought. It's not designed to join already established organisms, so when it moves into an older child, it causes some pain and temporary disability. The older the subject, the worse the effect. At a guess, no adult will ever survive the transition, and at another guess, the older the adult, the quicker he or she will succumb once critical mass is attained.

"I grant you, this theory has its rough edges, but it seems to fit the facts. Now, you were saying?"

"The little ones — Aled, Emilia, Vanessin and even Farne. None of them was affected before. And Finn and Claire had already survived the racking — the transition."

"That probably means the adaptation is permanent and requires constant reinforcement. Once a tadpole becomes a frog, it needs to breathe oxygen thereafter and use its legs to swim rather than a tail. There's no going back."

"Then we need to get the rest of the children down on that planet *now*."

"Yes. If we don't, I suspect we'll lose them all."

"But what about Ambassador Singh?"

"He wasn't wearing an iso-suit on his first visit to the surface. Did any of the techs take theirs off? Maybe to be more manoeuvrable when they went into the ship to check the Terra-tat and other systems?"

"I have no idea."

"If so, I think we can assume they'll die within a day or so at the most. I don't see any treatment being effective. The only safe thing is not to enter the transition at all."

"Do you think it's communicable? Dorothea and I, and one of the Provosts, all had close physical contact with one or more of the victims. Then there's whoever retrieved Ambassador Singh. Where was he, anyway?"

"In Passim Dee's room. He's the metallurgist."

"Were they together?"

"Dee went down in the lander with Ambassador Singh on Day One."

"We can assume he's dead, then — unless he was in an iso-suit?"

"I don't know. I'll get Talman to try to contact him. If he's still alive, we can warn him not to take that suit off under any circumstances."

Daffodil thought quickly. "We'll have to change plans — again. Doctor Suchet and one of the Provosts were taking the lander with another comm-set for young Edsen. We'll have to scrap that and make a mass descent, getting children down there as quickly as possible."

"That might be enough to save them as long as the other variables don't kick in to change things."

"What variables? We know it takes male and female, and different ethnicities."

"I can think of two. I'll give you a hint. How do you know the full names of the two babies with such precision? I doubt they could have told you."

"We got the names from the older ship-born and then used a laser-identifier to mark them. Oh. And we also immunised them all for common diseases to protect them back on Shiva or Terra. Surely that couldn't do any harm? They're Terran stock."

Harry Fejoa shrugged. "Who knows? They're not strictly Terran anymore. Immunising them could have changed the balance achieved after the first bout." He put his hand on her shoulder. "Don't blame yourself, Doctor Lan. Hindsight is a wonderful thing. If I'd had foresight instead, I'd be a happy old man with a wife and family."

Old man indeed. He was older than she was, yes, but old? She said impulsively, "Make that Daffodil. Daff. Let's not stand on formality anymore . . . Harry."

CHAPTER FOUR: ALMOST ALL?

Surface of Elydia. Shiptime 18 8 11. Elydia date 13 01 01
Edsen Balm

The lander was coming down, as Bede had reported. For a few seconds after Marianne and Edsen emerged from the animal hatch, it felt like déjà vu. The lander loomed larger as it dropped towards the Elydian surface.

Edsen poked at the unresponsive comm-set. Something must have gone wrong for the *Indira* to be back so soon. Or had it never left? He got a brief spurt of life from the gadget, but halfway through his request to speak with Jameel Singh, it went back into its electronic coma.

"Maybe Claire or the Causeways changed their minds, and they're coming back," Sherry suggested hopefully.

"We'll know in a few minutes." Marianne sounded tense. Edsen assumed she was afraid of more persuasions or reasoning to get more of them to go to Terra. There were so few of the *Top Enders* as they'd begun to refer to themselves. Just six of them were over fourteen.

By now, they knew the lander had a sensor that allowed it to choose a safe spot to put down, so Edsen simply stayed where he was, watching and waiting for the flip, bounce and extrusion of the balancing legs.

This certainty of safety made it all the more astonishing when the lander flipped twice, lolled in the air and fell like a dropped stone. Children screamed and fled, and Edsen must have dropped the comm-set, for the next thing he was aware of was standing several metres away clutching Marianne around the waist, hugging her against him like a treasure.

Flid! He was losing time again! "S-sorry," he stammered, getting her balanced and stepping back.

Marianne disregarded his apology. Her eyes were wide, and she grabbed his arm. "Wait!"

He hadn't been going anywhere.

"It crashed!" There was real fear in her voice.

They gazed at the lander, propped askew on the one leg that had unfolded.

"I think they're all right," he said. The lander wasn't right, but neither was it crushed and broken.

Marianne relaxed her grip and took a cautious step forward. Edsen went with her.

Together, they came to the lopsided craft and peered in through the bit of the transparent band they were able to reach.

It was difficult to see clearly, for there seemed to be people in a pile, but as they watched, two figures in iso-suits unfolded and started checking the other occupants, many of whom were crying with fear or indignation.

"The babies are back," Marianne murmured, sounding shocked.

She pulled away from Edsen and grasped at the door, trying to open it. It seemed stuck, or maybe it was fastened from the inside.

One of the suited figures wrestled with the door, and it opened with a screech. Seeing a small girl about to fall, Edsen stretched out his arms and plucked Amrita Kavya to safety.

The last time he'd seen her, she'd been holding Jameel Singh's hand, so he looked for Jameel. He wasn't one of the suited figures. One was too short, and the other had a mass of rose-pink showing within the helmet.

Amrita was wailing with fear and discomfort, so Edsen looked about for someone to look after her. When no one appeared, he yelled, "Elves."

That worked. Two girls and a boy dead-heated and Amrita held out her arms to one of the girls who gave her a cuddle and asked if she wanted to see a pool full of ducks.

Afterwards, Edsen wasn't sure if that really happened. It seemed unlikely. At the time, it was logical enough, as he became involved in a human chain of Noahs and Elves, passing small children from hand to hand until they found someone to recognise and cling to. That person then dropped out of the chain and went off with the returned child.

A dozen children were parcelled out, and then the suited figures climbed down. One of them, whom Edsen now recognised as Doctor Dorotea Suchet, reached into a pouch in her suit and handed him a new comm-set.

"What happened to the other one, Edsen?"

He shrugged, looking in wonder at the person in pink. "Who's that?"

"I don't know, exactly. Provost Rose is what she calls herself."

Edsen looked down at the new comm-set. "I dropped the other one when you crashed," he said.

"But it wasn't working anyway?"

"No. It went wrong. I don't think I did anything to it, but I need to ask Jameel if he knows how to fix it. Is he coming down? And why are you here? We thought you'd gone."

Doctor Suchet took his arm in her heavily-gloved hand. "Can we go somewhere quieter? I need to talk to you and Marianne."

He looked about and saw Marianne with Momo. He caught her eye and waved her over. The three of them walked towards the woolwood trees, which screened some of the noise.

They sat down, and Marianne hugged her knees and said, "What's going on, Doctor Dora?"

Doctor Suchet was silent, maybe organising her thoughts. Without being able to see her expression or, indeed, what she looked like, it was impossible to know what those thoughts might be.

"Why did you bring the kids back?" Edsen asked.

When she still didn't answer, he tapped the new comm-set.

"Please state your name and required contact."

Edsen spoke clearly, giving his newly decided designation. "Comm-set *Keeper* Edsen Balm from Elydia. I require contact with Ambassador Jameel Singh on *Indira*."

The response was unexpected. "I cannot comply with your request. Please state an alternative contact."

Edsen frowned. "Can I speak with Citizen Meera Singh, Tower—" He stopped short as Doctor Suchet reached over and tapped the screen to sleep mode.

"Flid! What'd you do that for?"

"I have some things to tell you before you contact Citizen Singh."

"Tell us then," Edsen said.

"First, I have a few questions for you both." She must have seen his annoyance because she held up a hand. "Please, bear with me. This is important. I'm not trying to waste your time."

"Go on then," Marianne said.

"Have you all been healthy since we left?"

"You weren't gone for long, and I told the man who contacted us earlier that we were fine," Edsen reminded.

"We're all well," Marianne cut in. She sounded a bit surprised.

"There haven't been any more cases of the racking?"

"No, thank flid." *Surely that was obvious? They wouldn't be calling themselves well, otherwise!*

"And you've had no after-effects. No soreness, nausea? You haven't been confused, or lost any time you can't account for?"

Edsen considered his recent grab for Marianne. He couldn't remember doing it, but he didn't think he'd lost time, exactly. It was more as if his body reacted to danger before his mind got working. If something looked as if it was falling on Marianne, of course, his body would grab her out of the way and run. His mind could thank him for it afterwards.

"We're well," Marianne said with determination.

"What do you have to tell us?" Edsen enquired, raising the comm-set in what he hoped was a resolute manner.

"There's no easy way to say this, but some of the children we took aboard *Indira* suffered bad reactions to their new environment."

"So that's why you brought some of them back," Marianne said.

"We're bringing almost all of them back because it seems likely there will be more bad reactions if we don't. We apologise to you and your people. The harm happened on our watch, but it wasn't intentional."

Edsen replayed her speech in his mind, frowning, and then picked out the important part. "*Almost all?* What about the others? Are they still going with you when you leave?"

Doctor Suchet spread her gauntleted hands. "I'm so sorry, but seven of your people have died. It happened with almost no warning. As soon as we realised what was happening, we returned as promptly as we could to bring the rest — home."

"Who? How?" Marianne's voice was soft, but it sent a prickle along Edsen's spine.

"It was the condition you call *the racking*. It came on suddenly and didn't respond to treatment."

"Who?" Marianne repeated.

"The first was Claire Atlantis, and then Finn Causeway." She paused, as if giving them time to absorb the information.

Edsen heard Marianne's sharp gasp. He thought he might have gasped himself. Claire and Finn! He felt genuine sorrow and a sense of loss for what had been going to happen, for the continued contact and the information they were going to share.

"But they had the racking and got better!" Marianne protested.

Edsen, watching her face, saw her eyes flash silver and her cheeks glitter suddenly. There was no pink flush, as he used to see sometimes when she exchanged *that* look with Jeremiah, but she was clearly agitated . . . and no wonder.

"Not this time, Marianne. It was over in minutes."

Marianne drew in a jerky breath, and Edsen moved closer to her and grabbed her hand. He wasn't sure what he feared . . . maybe that she'd start screaming as she had when she learned of Jeremiah's death. She controlled herself, though.

"Who else?" he asked. His mouth felt numb. There was surely no one else old enough, or had their theory been wrong all along?

"Farne Causeway. Doctor Lan and the Provost Rose made heroic efforts to save him, but he didn't respond to treatment. The others were Aled Kassia, Emilia Ocean, Vanessin Wilg and Tarn Rush. We hope and trust returning the rest to the planet will reverse the effect and no more will die. The shuttles are on their way."

There was a chill pause, and then Marianne turned and beckoned to Momo and Sakura and Hillman Hope, the only other Top-Ender not tending to a baby. "You need to hear this!"

They came over, solemn-faced, and Edsen noticed Momo's long black eyelashes seemed touched with silver.

"I think the Terrans know what causes the racking," Marianne said to the Moon blossoms. To Doctor Suchet, she said, "Please explain so we can understand. And please write this down in a data-book. Momo, do you have one? Hill, would you go and get one to record this, too?"

Hillman Hope loped off, while Momo produced a book from her shirt pocket, along with a pencil so new and sharp it must have come from the daily stores very recently. She offered these to Doctor Suchet.

"I usually make my case notes verbally."

"We need it written," Marianne said, as Hill tore back with a data-book he'd got from a shelter.

He flopped down cross-legged, prepared to start writing.

The medic took the pencil somewhat clumsily from Momo and opened the book, and then said, "The racking is a complex reaction to a physical transition. You've noticed the silver substance so abundant on this planet?"

"We call this place Elydia," Edsen said. He still had hold of Marianne's hand, but he felt her withdrawing from him as she slipped into organisation mode. She moved her hand as if to rub her wrist, and he let it slip from his.

Doctor Suchet nodded acknowledgement.

"We don't know exactly what the substance is, but it seems a systemic part of the ecology here."

"What does that have to do with the racking, Doctor Suchet?" Momo asked.

"We believe the substance is bound up in the plants at a cellular level. It's in the ground, the water, and the air. If there are any indigenous animals here . . . That means animals you didn't bring with you on the ship . . ."

"Jameel said there were small ones and big ones. He contacted us and told us to be careful. Ask him about that," Edsen said.

"Any indigenous animals would be born with the silver substance in their systems and would ingest more through normal means their whole life through. Unfortunately for you, it's a much more difficult job to acclimatise to it later in life. The smaller children had a largely trouble-free transition, but the older you are, the more difficult it is, and at some point, it becomes impossible."

"I see. That's why Marianne was the worst . . . I mean, the worst who didn't die," Momo said.

"What happened to Claire and the others then? Did you try to get the stuff out of them?" Marianne sounded accusing.

"No. We expected the silver colour would fade when they were no longer exposed to it. You have carrots, don't you?"

"Yes. Do I write that down?" Hill sounded surprised.

"Write *everything*," Marianne said.

"Carrots contain a substance called beta-carotene. That's what makes a lot of them orange. If light-skinned people eat a great many carrots, the palms of their hands will go yellow. If they cut back on the carrots, the colour goes away. We thought that would happen with the silvering, but we now believe your people have become physically dependent on having it in their systems. Doctor Benz suggests the transition is one-way and permanent," Doctor Suchet said.

"I suppose that means losing it is as bad as getting it. No, worse, since it hit the little ones," Edsen said, wincing.

Momo said, politely, "Do you think the little ones you've brought back will be all right, Doctor Suchet?"

"I do hope so, Momo. We all felt it was too risky to keep any of them on *Indira*, let alone try to get them to Shiva or Terra."

"What should we do if the ones who come back *do* get the racking?"

Doctor Suchet put down the pencil and turned out her

hands. "We have no viable treatment. We can only hope the return will stop the withdrawal effect."

She passed the book back to Momo.

Hill went on scribbling for a minute more and then handed the data-book and pencil to Edsen. "Check this through, would you? It's a bit mixed up." It certainly was, but Hill had clear writing and Edsen could see the facts were there. He wondered if Sherry would get carrots to grow in the garden she was planning. If she did, would they be orange or silver?

"We can copy it out in the proper order later," Marianne said, apparently overhearing.

"Doctor Suchet, why did the silver hurt some people so much if it is just part of everything here?" Sakura asked.

"That's difficult to explain. It seems to want to become part of your cells. Do you know what cells are?"

"Our mother said they were the small pieces that make up bodies," Momo said.

"That's right. Saying *want* makes it seem as if the silver is alive, but we don't think it is. It just *is* part of everything on this planet. It makes its way into your lungs when you breathe, and into your bodies when you eat fruit that grows here or drink the water. It also bonds with your joints and bones, and that's probably what made it hurt."

"Are we going to be all right now?" Edsen asked.

"Again, we don't know, but I think you probably will be."

"As long as we never leave Elydia," Marianne said. She didn't sound triumphant.

"Well, yes. But in terms of human history, it's only in very recent times that there's been the choice of living anywhere but Terra. It's only just over three hundred years since humans landed on any other body, and that was Luna. No one ever thought we could live there and indeed, fifty years after that first landing only twelve people had walked on the surface. The first *habitable* body wasn't settled until eighteen years ago."

"Luna Sunflower is the name of one of our little ones. Sol's little sister. I didn't know it was a *place,*" Sakura said.

"Luna is the single moon of Terra. Sol is the name of Terra's star. I suppose their parents must have known that when they named them."

"Moon is our family name." Sakura still looked puzzled.

Marianne was frowning, and Edsen wondered why. She didn't want to leave Elydia. She hadn't, right from the start. So, why would hearing they never could seem to bother her?

He soon found out.

Still scowling, she said, "How do you know the silver gets into our bones?" She lifted her slim arm and turned it to examine her wrist, bending her hand back and forth.

There was another pause. Edsen got the feeling Doctor Suchet didn't want to answer.

"You can't see bones. They're inside you," he prompted. He wanted to hold Marianne's wrist and feel the supple way it moved and the steady pulse of life under the skin. He remembered that wrist had been swollen and hurting, but now it looked even better than new.

"So, how can you know?" he persisted.

"You do an autopsy," Doctor Suchet said.

"Our mother said that meant cutting dead bodies to see what went wrong, only of course no one on *Elysian Dawn* died until the crash," Momo said.

"No one at *all* died?" Doctor Suchet sounded nonplussed.

"Hanaka said a lot of things that make people die on Terra just couldn't happen to us. She had a whole list of things she said made people on Terra sick. She'd never seen most of them in our people, but she kept the list to pass down to the *Heirs.*"

"I see."

"So you did autopsy on Finn and the others," Edsen said, not liking the idea of chopping his friends up as if they'd been carrots.

"Doctor Benz did, yes. Doctor Fejoa assisted him. We hoped to find out what happened and whether we could stop it happening to anyone else. We found the silver had gone right through their systems. It must have begun soon after you crashed. You couldn't have avoided it, once the ship's hull integrity was gone."

"The air and the water and fruit have all done this to us," Marianne said. She looked grim, and Edsen saw she was squeezing her hands together until the knuckles shone pale. "We didn't know. I tasted the food and thought it was all right because it didn't burn my mouth. I tried drinking from the pondcups and told everyone it was all right. I told Moon it was all right, and she agreed. She did some tests and didn't find anything dangerous. I even got Jem to taste things. And so, he died."

"Marianne, you couldn't possibly have known. And in any case, there was nothing you could have done, even if you'd never eaten any fruit or drunk the native water. You'd already breathed the air, all of you, when the ship cracked open."

Marianne turned her sombre gaze to the medic. "Will you be all right? When you leave here, I mean?"

"I believe so. I've worn an iso-suit from the start."

There was another pause, and then Marianne said abruptly, "Ambassador Singh is dead, isn't he?"

Chapter Five: They're Children!

Surface of Elydia. Elydia date 13 01 01
Doctor Dorotea Suchet

Dorotea groaned inwardly. Of course, they had to guess. These teenagers were descended from healthy, intelligent, adventurous people. Of course, they were going to work out the obvious conclusion.

"And I told him it was safe to come out of the lander." Marianne Arcadia was stone-faced.

"You couldn't have known. There was *nothing* to tell you the air was—" She broke off, not wanting to say *harmful* or *lethal*. All she could do was to reiterate what was, after all, the truth.

"He asked if it was all right and I said it was! I thought he was being silly for asking."

Dorotea leaned forward. "Marianne, Ambassador Singh was an intelligent adult. It was his own choice to come out of the lander wearing ship clothing instead of an iso-suit."

"He put on a long white thing," Edsen muttered.

Dorotea saw he was feeling shaken. He'd formed a working relationship with the young ambassador even if it hadn't warmed into friendship.

"That wasn't an iso-suit. It was a burnous. It's the clothing Shivan residents and Citizens wear outdoors. Their sunlight is so strong it can kill from quite a brief exposure." She paused, and added, "You see, there is danger on other planets. There are places on Terra, which is the cradle of our race, where no human can survive unassisted for more than a day at the most. Death Valley, or Antarctica, or the top of Mount Everest, or the Mariana Trench . . . all killers in their way. Obviously, every planet we settle is going to have its challenges and its dangers. From what I see here, your new home has a pleasant climate, at least at this time of year. You have fresh water, fruit and — great God! What is *that*?" Of course, she knew perfectly well what it was. She just hadn't expected to see a half-grown parti-coloured lamb on a planet so far from Terra.

"That's called a sheep. It's a Terran animal," the girl named Momo said.

"Two sheep," Edsen corrected as a harlequin lamb appeared through the strange woolly bushes.

Woolly bushes. Lambs. Naturally, they'd feel at home here, Dorotea thought. She felt a trifle hysterical.

"How long have they been here? And what's that brown stuff on the wool?" she asked, watching as the first lamb came up to nudge the youngest girl. Sakura, her name was, and she was clearly Momo's sister. She looked about ten.

"The Noahs got them out of the tanks yesterday and today," the child said, giggling as the lamb lipped at her sleeve.

Noahs? She supposed it made sense. "But surely you didn't have flocks of sheep on the ship?"

She could understand gardens, but livestock would have been far more difficult to maintain.

Edsen said, "They were in tanks, in brown goopy stuff that kept them asleep until we got to Magellan Sixteen. Now we're staying here instead, and the systems went wrong. The techs who looked at the Terra-tattle went to see them, and Terror said they wouldn't live much longer in the tanks, so Marianne said we should get them out and let them have a chance."

Terror? Oh yes, the tech whose parents must have had a pun-

*ning mindset when they named him Terrence Australis. No won-
der people called him* Terror. *It was inevitable.*

"We do hope they don't get the racking," Momo said.

"I think I can set your minds at rest on that." For the first
time in a couple of days, Dorotea smiled, though of course
she knew they couldn't see her face clearly. "That's if they're
all this size? This age?"

"The horses are bigger. They come up to my chest! The
goats are this size, and the hens and ducks are a bit fluffy
and small with funny hair," Sakura said.

"Then I think they'll be fine. They're young, you see." She
saw they didn't really understand. "I mean, they're children.
Only we call them lambs and kids, foals and chicks and
ducklings. Hens and ducks have feathers, by the way. We
don't call it hair."

"Feathers," the boy named Hill muttered, writing it
down.

"That's it. Spell it with an a after the first e. And oh, yes, I
think your animals will be safe from the racking, although
I'm not sure they're safe from other things. What are you
planning to do with them? Are they just going to wander
about? Are you going to use their manure as fertiliser? Or
milk the goats?"

"We don't know yet. We just wanted them to have a
chance at living," Marianne said.

"We don't know anything about them, except that some
people ride on horses and wool comes from sheep," Momo
said.

"And now we know ducks and hens have feathers," Hill
said.

"You don't know *any* more?" Dorotea was amazed at the
patches of extreme ignorance in these otherwise intelligent
and articulate adolescents.

Momo lifted one shoulder. "They were meant to stay in
the tanks until long after we were dead. The animal *Keepers*

and *Heirs* knew more, and they would have passed it on until it was needed, but they're all dead."

"Great God!"

"We hope there might be some things written down in the stores, but those are all messed up," Momo added.

Dorotea saw why they were so determined to have things written down. Presumably, they didn't have any electronic recorders. That was part of the future-proofing. Acid-free paper could be burned or destroyed by water, but otherwise, properly stored, it might last for centuries.

"I'll write down everything I know about looking after animals and send it down to you via the lander," she offered impulsively. She was no farmer or grazier, but she could pool information with the crew and get printouts from the vast databrain on *Indira*. It was dawning on her that although these children could never leave their planet, they need not be unsupported. She could arrange for regular information updates to be sent to them, either as physical books dropped off by anyone out this way in future—or by reports sent via the comm-set. Only there must be more than one comm-set on the planet, and more people trained to use them. Even supposedly fail-proof gadgets could fail. The lander's land-legs were a case in point.

She sighed, hoping a tech from one of the shuttles could fix the legs before the next trip down.

The girls and the scribing boy seemed pleased with her offer, but the other boy turned a solemn face to her.

"What is it, Edsen?"

"Finn and Claire were going to tell us things like that using the comm-set. So was Jameel. Will someone still do that for us?"

"I was just thinking about that." She remembered as she spoke that *Indira* might never be able to land anywhere, but now they'd identified the source of the racking, she hoped they could use a vacuum-dump to remove any vestiges of the silver substance from the ship, including the waste system. The double-airlock system of the lander and shuttles should have rendered it safe from contamination. In fact, the only source of danger lay in the dead bodies on *Indira*. These must be brought down to the planet as quickly as possible. No doubt Citizen Singh would want her brother's body returned to Shiva, but that couldn't happen.

The hairs on her neck rose in a *frisson* of horror at the thought of the silver substance in Jameel Singh's bones, lungs and gut leaching out into the soil of Shiva if he was buried there. Then she remembered that was unlikely, as Terra-born residents' bodies were cremated and returned to Terra.

Oh. Even cremation could have its dangers. Who knew if fire would destroy the substance that had killed him? Some things didn't burn. If that silvering got loose . . .

She almost laughed. The Shivan Citizens couldn't leave their planet in any case, and most of them were young enough to survive the racking, or not to get it at all. Such a leak would affect the Terra-born visitors and long-term residents, but that would be all. It would simply hasten the Provosts' plan by a few years. If it got into the Terran system, which it would when all those bodies were expelled, it would have an even more catastrophic effect. After a generation or so, no Terran would be able to leave the planet.

She realised the five ship-born were looking at her expectantly. *Keep your mind on the job*, she told herself severely. She wasn't usually scatter-brained, and the death of billions of Terra-born and Terrans was certainly no laughing matter.

"I need to go and help bring the children out of the shuttles," she said, getting up.

The five ship-born got up, too, with the ease of unencumbered youth. Dorotea was unhappily aware of her aging joints and the heavy iso-suit. She wasn't the one with lethal silver lodged in her joints! She'd never know the feel of the air and sun on Elydia. "This will take a while, but will you think about the information you want? Write it down, Hill . . . no, tell me! I'll see what I can give you."

Nearly slipped up there, Dora! she informed herself and shuddered again. What if she'd taken paper requests back to *Indira* and the paper had been contaminated with the silver substance? Paper was organic. She *must* be more careful!

Marianne Arcadia

It was good to know the animals would probably be all right. Marianne had never thought of how old they were, assuming they were adults. The information Doctor Suchet promised would be useful. They'd still search for any documents the animal *Keepers* had left in storage, but it would be useful to ask questions of an adult who was willing to answer them. If only the Terra-born on *Elysian Dawn* had talked freely! *They* had remembered animals. The knowledge in their heads would have been so valuable.

"I'm sorry about Ambassador Singh," she said to Edsen.

"So am I. And I suppose the other man, Passim Dee, has died, too."

"I expect so." Marianne thought of the cheerful person who'd gone off exploring their planet. "I wonder what happened to that thing he had with him."

"What thing? The comm-set?"

"No. It was like the Celestial map, but it showed places here, not in space. Remember, I told you he had one?"

Edsen nodded. "I remember. I was sorry I didn't get a look at it, but I was learning to use the comm-set. Maybe we can find it. Or maybe Doctor Suchet will give us one. That's something to ask for."

A lull in the noise around the ship made them stop and peer upwards as the first of the shuttles loomed down into view. Remembering what happened to the lander, they backed up against *Elysian Dawn* for safety, but the shuttle flipped and bounced, landed neatly and folded down.

Doctor Suchet and the Rose Provost approached the ship, and there was a general surge after them.

"I hope they're all right. We never should have let them go," Marianne said. She thought of Claire. She hadn't been the most helpful of people, but she'd been likable enough. Her mind shied away from Finn and Farne. Finn had been the nearest to her in age, and Farne was a friend of Aleph's. She groaned under her breath. She'd have to tell Aleph. He'd be waiting for Farne to come out of the shuttle.

The door opened smoothly, and someone in an iso-suit stepped out, leading two children by the hands. Marianne noticed there was a shorter-than-usual pause before they came out. Evidently, the people from *Indira* had decided they could do no more harm to Elydia than they had already. Or maybe, she thought, trying to be charitable, they wanted to get the children back to safety as quickly as they could.

Three more suited adults came out with more children. The ones who were five or six seemed uncertain, looking about until they found faces they recognised. The small ones were subdued. Was it imagination, or were their skins an unhealthy colour? The silver sheen was faded and greyish.

Marianne turned to Momo. "I think we need to get them to the washing pool. Since the water has the silver in it, they might feel better straight away."

Momo moved off to organise the Elves.

Marianne just hoped the pool wasn't full of ducks. *Duck-lings,* she corrected herself. That's what Doctor Suchet called them. They were fun to watch, but they did spend a lot of time in the pool. Maybe they could find another pool for washing? Or build a kind of wall?

The shuttle was empty, and the adults, all but Doctor Suchet, went back inside. This time they did take the time to stand and wait, move, stand and wait.

"What are they doing?" she asked.

"It's called decontamination. It sucks all the pollen and dust and bits and pieces off our iso-suits and pumps it back into your atmosphere."

Marianne drew her brows together. "It wouldn't work with the silver that's inside us though."

"No." The doctor drew a couple of breaths as if she meant to say something.

"What is it?" Marianne asked.

"When the last of the children are down, we'll bring back Claire and the others. I think you'll want to bury them with their families?"

"There are so many to be buried already." Marianne knew she sounded abrupt, but this was something that had been troubling her. She'd thought they might close *Elysian Dawn* and leave the lost ones where they were, but there were still thousands of things in the stores to sort out. The job had been intended for a much larger group than they were, and no one had thought the ship would crash, jumbling everything together.

"I know." Doctor Suchet sounded sad.

Marianne watched at the shuttle leapt skywards. She was tired of sorrow and tired of making decisions. She'd so resented it when Anya refused to let her marry Jeremiah immediately. She still did, but she missed having someone to suggest and direct and to tell her what she should do. Momo, Edsen and Tamma were capable people. So were Sherry and the other Top-Ender boys. They were younger, though, and they tended to defer to her. She'd have to find someone to direct the Elves. Momo, maybe. She wasn't much older than they were, but she was strong and dependable.

Yes. Momo was the right choice. Marianne remembered, with shame, how Momo and the other Moon blossoms had taken charge in the wake of the disaster. What had she done? Shrieked and tried to die, because Jeremiah was gone, and she didn't want to go on without him.

Still looking up, she said, "We have so many to put in the earth. It will take us a long time."

"And it's not a job that should fall to children. It's possible some of the techs from *Indira* will be able to help you. Now that we don't have the second trip to make, we might be able to spend that time down here and help you with the burials."

"Isn't that dangerous for you?"

"I don't see why it should be if we're all careful. In any case, we will take care of the burial for Ambassador Singh."

"I suppose you can't take him home. And there's the other man, Passim Dee."

Suchet nodded soberly. She focused on the Elves. "What are you doing with the children we brought down? They should probably rest."

"We're taking them to the pool. They like that, and it will make them better, I think." Marianne felt the need for advice receding. These people meant well, but their *help* had brought more deaths on the Elydians.

"You are probably right. Do you mind if I go along and watch to see how they are affected? I promise I won't interfere."

"Aph will take you." Marianne beckoned, then said hastily, "Farne was a friend of Aph's. Please don't . . ."

The doctor murmured agreement.

Marianne watched the clumsily-suited figure heading away towards the pool with her brother. She realised there was more to organise. They'd have nearly a hundred more younger children to feed and care for. That meant more food to be gathered. She remembered Sherry wanted to plant some of the seed stock from *Elysian Dawn* in the Elydian soil. She wondered if it would grow, and how the vegetables would taste if they did grow. Would beans still be beans?

CHAPTER SIX: CHICKEN AND EGG

Surface of Elydia. Elydia date 13 01 01
Edsen Balm

The second shuttle came down and disgorged more children and two suited technicians who went straight to the lopsided lander.

Edsen followed. He still wanted to contact Citizen Singh and get her to let Cornelia from Outward-Bound know what was happening. He thought someone from *Indira* had probably done that already, but he was the com-tat, and it was his duty to explain why the rescue hadn't worked as planned.

The only reason he hadn't made the contact already was because he wasn't sure what to say about Ambassador Singh. Citizen Singh was an imperious and rather frightening person, but she had just lost her brother, and he knew how unhappy she must feel.

He wished he had someone to ask. Since he didn't, he went to watch what the techs did to fix the lander.

They wouldn't let him inside.

"Sorry, son. We need to keep the silver stuff out," one said.

Edsen pointed out they'd just brought children to the planet who had as much of the silver stuff in their systems as he had.

They shook their heads and said they had their orders. Unfortunately, the tech called *Terror* Australis wasn't among them. He mightn't have let Edsen in either, but he would have been friendlier, and he wouldn't have called him *son*.

Grumpily, Edsen sat down to wait. If they wouldn't show him, they could tell him. Then he realised they probably wouldn't come out but would fix the lander and then take off back for *Indira*.

He retreated to the second shuttle. That was closed and flexing up its land-legs, ready to leave. Edsen watched it pounce upwards and blinked. Was that a wobble? A hesitation? He was sure the shuttle hung in the air and tilted a little before it righted itself and rose out of sight.

"Did you see that?" he asked Marianne, who had also watched the take-off.

"What?"

"A wobble."

"Was that a wobble? I thought it was just heading up to match orbits with *Indira*. Ed, Sherry wants to put in some of the seedstock. I'll help her, but we need some tools. Do you know where the spades were put after we buried the first lost ones?"

"They're just inside the first door. Do you want them now?"

"Yes. I'm tired of waiting for these Terrans to finish what they're doing and go. Doctor Suchet said some of the techs might help us with the burials, but we have other things to do as well."

"They wouldn't let me watch them fix the lander," Edsen growled.

Her frown came back. "They're taking a long time with it. Are you going to get them to fix the other comm-set?"

"Good idea, if I can find it. It must be somewhere near the lander."

"It might be underneath it. I think we were standing about there when you grabbed me out of the way."

He grinned. "Sorry about that."

"I'm not. I didn't get through the crash and the racking to be squashed by a lander. We'd better look for the comm-set."

They walked back to the lander. As they approached, it lurched as the one extended leg started to fold and then stuck. They backed away.

Behind them, the next shuttle came down with its load, and two more technicians entered the lander.

The last children came back on the shuttle after that, and their attendants gave them over to the Elves. Two suited figures came over to stand by Marianne and Edsen.

"Marianne?"

She swung around.

"I think that's Doctor Lan," Edsen whispered.

Marianne gestured her thanks. "Doctor Lan?"

"Yes. We wanted to tell you how very sorry we are for your loss."

"Doctor Suchet said that, too. We don't blame you."

The word *much* hovered in the air, and Edsen hurried in to block it. "After all, Eduard . . . my father . . . reported the crash to Outward-Bound. If he hadn't . . ." Edsen lost track of his thought for a few seconds and then continued, "Well, if he hadn't, then no one would have known we weren't still travelling . . . not until the next report was due. Most of us would still be dead anyway. And we wouldn't know sheep that are children are called lambs or that ducks and hens have feathers and not hair."

Marianne stuck her elbow in his ribs. "I think that's enough, Ed."

"No, I understand what you mean. It's just a string of things that happened," the other person said. Edsen saw his suit badge said he was Doctor H. Fejoa.

"We can't undo the things that happened, but we want

you to know you can always call on us if you need advice or practical help. We won't be able to get to you the next day, but we'll arrange what we can," Doctor Lan said.

"That will be useful. The first thing we need to know is how to fix the comm-set that went wrong."

"When we find it, that is," Marianne put in.

"I don't have my tools here, but we'll get one of the techs to help you," Fejoa said.

"They can mend just about anything," Doctor Lan said.

"Except that lander, evidently." Doctor Fejoa waved his hand it that direction. He moved up closer and peered in through the transparent band, then turned back, shaking his head. "Never heard of land-legs malfunctioning like that."

"It went wrong before it landed. It came down out of control and crashed," Edsen pointed out.

"Are you sure?"

"We saw it happen. Ask Doctor Suchet. She was inside it."

"Sounds like a chicken and egg situation." Maybe he saw they didn't understand the idiom, because he clarified, "Did it crash because the land-legs failed, or did the land-legs fail because it crashed?"

Edsen, not knowing how land-legs worked, shrugged.

They waited for a while longer. Edsen wanted to get the garden tools for Marianne, but he also wanted the lander to move so he could look for the comm-set. After a bit, he turned to the doctors. "What kind of medics are you? Doctor Suchet said she knows most about children. Doctor Benz knows about bones and insides. What about you?"

"I'm a general practitioner. That means I know a fair bit about a lot of things, and I'm still learning," Doctor Lan said.

"I specialise in exotic diseases and counselling," Doctor Fejoa added.

"What's counselling?"

"When challenging situations come up, I try to help people through them with suggestions. I should add your situation is about the most challenging I've ever heard of."

"You might be able to help me then."

"I can try, but I think you're doing well already. Much better than I would. Actually, much better than I *did* when my most challenging situation struck."

"I'm all right. I want to contact Citizen Meera Singh at Krishna Tower two, though."

"You can do that through your comm-set. The one that works."

"I know, but Jameel was her brother, and he died because he came to rescue us. That happened because Outward-Bound asked for help and *that* happened because Eduard sent out a report to say what happened to us. Do you think she'll be angry with me?"

"I do know the Citizen, but I can't say how she'll feel about this. It would be unreasonable of her to be angry with you, but people, even Shivan Citizens, can be unreasonable. May I ask why you want to talk to her?"

Edsen flipped back his hair. It was difficult remembering who knew what. Jameel would have known this.

Marianne explained before he could untangle it. "Ed is our com-tat. *Elysian Dawn* com-tats have a duty to make regular reports to Outward-Bound, and Ed is the only one left. Since the Terra-tat died, Ed has to use this comm-set, and Outward-Bound don't have one. He makes his reports to Citizen Singh, and she passes them to Outward-Bound. She can talk to Ed *and* Cornelia Conti, but they can't talk to one another."

Edsen relaxed, grateful to hear it expressed so clearly.

"Quite a dilemma," Fejoa said.

Doctor Lan cut in, saying, "Why doesn't Outward-Bound just get a modern comm-set? That way Edsen can make his reports to them directly. That is, if he needs to make reports. The journey has ended, so we might argue the duty has ended with it."

"I want to let them know what's happening, anyway. Do you think you can talk to them about getting a comm-set when you're back on Terra?" Edsen said.

"Yes, if we ever get there." Lan sounded sad.

The other doctor patted the shoulder of her iso-suit. "We'll get there, Daff. None of us except for Jameel and the metallurgist ever got this stuff in our systems, and if we do a good filter-flush-and-purge as we leave the Caspar system, there shouldn't be a problem. What *are* they doing in that lander?"

Eventually, the techs emerged, saying they couldn't fix the land-legs because the mechanism had seized. "It'll have to take off as-is and get a thorough overhaul once we're back on Shiva," one of them said.

"Who flew the thing down here?" another one grumbled.

"It was a Provost called Rose this time. The time before it was Jameel and Passim Dee," Edsen told them.

They seemed surprised he'd spoken but stopped grumbling. Edsen wasn't sure if that was because Jameel and Dee were dead, or if the Provost was someone important and not to be criticised.

Now that he had their attention, he asked them how to repair the comm-set.

"You don't," one of them said.

"He means, they don't need it. They're just about bullet-proof," another clarified.

"My first one went wrong," Edsen pointed out, but they just shrugged and suggested he must have made a mistake while using it.

And that was the trouble with the people from *Indira*, Edsen thought. They had ideas and notions, and they knew how things ought to be. If they weren't that way, it took a lot of work to get them to stop believing what should be and get them to believe what *was*.

The lander took off, piloted by the Provost with the pink clothing inside the iso-suit. Edsen still wasn't clear what a Provost did, or even was, but he was more focused on retrieving his first comm-set, anyway. Nevertheless, he stayed well back until the lander disappeared. It wobbled a lot as it rose, and even the techs retreated to the shelter of *Elysian Dawn*.

Edsen went to the area of crushed vegetation where the lander had been. There was a gouge in the soil where the one land-leg had bitten in. It was quite deep, and Edsen wondered if that was a good place to put one of the garden plots Sherry and Marianne wanted. Sherry had already started one, but they needed more. The soil was greyish and crumbly, but when he scooped some up, it smelled almost the way soil should. His mouth watered as he visualised the carrots and potatoes they might grow. Harvest would be a few months off, but maybe the girls would find radish or cress seeds. Nasturtiums were good, too, and they could be eaten soon after planting.

The thought of growing familiar things was a cheerful one, and he was further cheered when one of the goats . . . a kid, he corrected himself mentally, came over and rubbed its face against his leg. Little Amrita followed it, and he encouraged her to touch the soft nose. The animal seemed to like that, and Edsen noticed the brown goop, now dry, was flaking off, leaving the hair underneath shiny and soft.

The kid wandered off, and Amrita turned her attention to Edsen, lifting her arms, clearly wanting him to pick her up. He did so, and she stroked his nose the way she had the kid's and giggled.

Then she leaned back and fixed him with wide silvery eyes. "Where Meel?"

"You're hungry? We can get some fruit."

"Meel!" She sounded imperious.

"We haven't got much else just yet."

"Where Meel? *Meel?*"

That's when it hit him. She was asking for Jameel Singh.

For a few seconds, Edsen felt tears fighting to fall. Loss tried to overwhelm him, but he took a deep breath and made a decision. He was alive and well, while so many others were dead. He wasn't going to waste this life in crying. He swung the little girl around and set her back on the silver grass. "Jameel isn't here anymore, Amrita. You'll have to put up with me instead." He pulled the comm-set out of his pocket and showed it to her, then pointed at the ground. "Can you find me something that looks just like this?"

The child cocked her head and moved off purposefully.

Edsen followed her about until he saw a square black shape nestled in the grass.

He waited while Amrita picked it up and showed it to him in triumph.

Edsen praised her for her cleverness, bent and gave her a spontaneous hug. He wasn't her dad or her brother. He wasn't even Jameel Singh. Whatever he was to her, he'd have to do.

Chapter Seven: "What They Need to Know"

Surface of Elydia. Elydia date 13 01 01
Marianne Arcadia

By the time darkness was falling, the folk from *Indira* had either returned to the ship or retreated to the remaining shuttle for the night. They sealed themselves in, and presumably ate and slept. Some of the Elves peered through the view screen and reported the people inside had removed their iso-suits.

Marianne was about to go and see what Doctor Suchet and the others looked like when Edsen called her.

She turned to see what he wanted and saw he was sitting with Bede and Amrita. The little girl was asleep, which meant Edsen had only one useful arm.

He peered up at her with the usual toss of his fringe. "Have a look at this, Mim."

"Mim?"

He said defensively, "That's what Aleph and Bede call you."

"I suppose so—Ed." She looked at the black devices side-by-side on the ground, illuminated by one of the candle-lanterns the resourceful Momo had discovered in the stores. "You found the first comm-set. Is it working now?"

"No."

"Those techs really did get it wrong. What did you want

to show me?"

"Bede said since it's broken, and the techs won't try to fix it, why shouldn't we look inside it. What do you think?"

"I think it's up to you. Jameel Singh gave it to you. One thing though, can you open it? Is there any way in?"

"There's a seam you can nearly get your thumbnail in," Edsen said, nodding to Bede, who demonstrated.

"And screws," Bede said.

"Have we got a screwdriver?"

"Not here, but there's some rock."

"That will just flake off," Marianne pointed out. She had mixed feelings about the silver rock. It had killed too many people, but now they needed it.

"This seed then." Bede delved in his pocket and pulled out three of the silver seeds from the melon they'd found.

"Isn't that too soft?" Marianne remembered biting one to test for solanine.

"Not now. They've dried out hard. You can use them to draw on rock. I'm calling them rockseeds, so we can call the melons rockmelons."

"I suppose you can try using one."

"You have a go, Bede. I'm a bit handicapped," Edsen said, nodding down towards the small child resting against him.

Marianne reflected that Amrita should have been in bed, but it was so much easier to let the little ones eat and sleep when they wanted. She decided to ask Doctor Suchet about that. She was an expert in small children. She turned her attention to her brother.

He got the broken comm-set gripped between his knees and pressed the wedge-shaped end of the seed into the slot of one of the screws. It took a fair while to get it angled properly, but Bede didn't give up. Marianne was about to ask if she could have a go when he exclaimed with satisfaction. "It's turning!"

Marianne thought he'd have to remove the screw on the other side as well, but Bede put down his makeshift screwdriver and gave the comm-set a sharp twist. One half swivelled away.

All three craned to see inside.

"It's almost empty," Bede said, puzzled.

"What's that black and silver bit?" Edsen reached out his free hand to indicate a small mass in the corner of the shell.

"Maybe that's the bit that makes it work?" Bede prodded it with his finger. "I think it's broken. Look. Is this supposed to be loose?" He lifted a bit of silver free and handed it to Edsen.

"How would I know?"

Marianne held out her hand, and Edsen dropped the small mass into her palm. She rolled it about. "This looks like the silver rock stuff. Maybe it got in there by mistake." She froze, as a nasty thought hit her. "Maybe it got in and killed the comm-set!"

"Something did," Edsen muttered. He looked at the undamaged one, resting on the ground, and picked it up. He touched the screen.

"Please state your name and required contact."

Marianne clenched her hands in relief as the expected voice came through. This one was still all right.

"Comm-set *Keeper* Edsen Balm from Elydia. I require contact with—" Edsen stopped short and glanced at Marianne. "Who?" he mouthed.

"Um . . . Commtech Talman. That's the man you talked to before, isn't it?"

He nodded. "Commtech Talman on *Indira*."

"Talman here." The response came promptly, and Marianne saw a man with sandy reddish hair appear on the screen. She moved to lean over Edsen's shoulder and saw the commtech's eyes flicker as he acknowledged her presence.

"The first comm-set—the one Ambassador Singh gave me—died while I was talking to you. Remember?"

"I remember. Is it working again?"

"No. This is a new one Doctor Suchet gave us. We opened the other one and found some silver stuff inside. Is that meant to be there?"

Talman smiled and shrugged. "I don't know, Edsen. I use them. I don't poke about inside them."

"Will you open one and see?"

"I'm not authorised to do that."

Marianne leaned closer. "Can you get authorised? Or do you want us to send up the broken one, so you can see for yourself?"

As she expected, the commtech said he certainly wasn't authorised to agree with that. As she hoped, he came up with an alternative solution.

"If you hold the broken set up to the screen, I can look at it that way. I don't know what good it will do, though."

Edsen complied, first replacing the bit of silver.

After a few moments of silent contemplation, Talman said he still had no idea. "But at least I'll know what this one looks like inside, so if I get authorisation to unscrew another one I can compare it."

That seemed as much as they were going to get. Edsen closed off the conversation and pocketed the comm-set.

"What are you going to do with that one?" Marianne indicated the broken device.

"I don't know. Put it somewhere safe, probably."

"If that silver is the same as the stuff we've got in our bones it might get bigger."

"I'll gauge it," Edsen said. He sighed audibly.

"What?" Marianne asked.

"Remember when I got gauged last, and Moon cut my

food back to get me onto the right percentile?"

"Yes. You were grumpy about it."

"Not as grumpy as you were about your extra centimetres."

Bede looked from one of them to the other. "Are we still going to get gauged?"

"I don't think so, Bede, unless Momo knows how to do it." Marianne smiled affectionately at him. "You're just right, anyway."

"Anya used to say that."

"I know. Anya and Markus would be happy to see you now." She knew she sounded awkward, and she wasn't sure what Anya would have made of her silver-eyed son, but she felt it was important for Bede to remember how it was to have parents, and how it was to be a child. "Will you go and get some fruit for Ed and me?" she asked abruptly.

"Bossy socks." Bede grinned at her but went off quite cheerfully.

"I could have got my own. Amrita ought to be in the shelter anyway," Edsen said.

"Yes, but I wanted to ask you something."

He frowned, and she hurried on, feeling more awkward by the moment. "I'm grown up. I mean, I was going to be marrying Jeremiah and living with him, so Anya and Markus wouldn't have been—you know?"

"I know."

"Finn was nearly grown-up, but everyone else was still . . ."

"Kids, having our rations cut when we got too heavy and our manners watched," Edsen put in. His frown deepened. "You don't have to look after us all, Mim."

"I know! Anyway, people like Momo and Tamma and some of the other Elves are better with the little kids than I am. What I mean is you Top-Ender boys—you and Granton and Zeb and Hill—you'll have to teach the little boys what they have to know to be men. What your fathers taught you. Things your mothers didn't tell you, I mean." She felt her cheeks warming with embarrassment.

Edsen seemed embarrassed, too, but he smiled. "Yes, I see. You realise we probably don't know much ourselves? We didn't even have our lists yet. Well, Finn might have . . ."

"No, but you must have asked your fathers or big brothers questions sometimes when things started happening to you. So when Bede and the others start asking, I want them to know who to go to. Otherwise, they'll get worried, or ask one another, and probably get it all wrong. Sherry and Momo and I will talk to the girls. Moon used to explain some things, but I don't know if she said the same things to you boys as she did to girls."

He said, "I'll talk to the others. Maybe we can get together with Aph and some of the Elves and find out what they know already and what they want to know. Then we can write it down, and then move down to the boys Bede's age. If we can get it all written in a data-book, it'll be there for the little kids and their kids . . . if they have any."

Marianne sighed. "Thanks, Ed. I could have asked Doctor Fejoa or the techs, but their lives are nothing like ours. And they're not going to be here for much longer. We need to depend on ourselves."

"Do you think they'll come back sometimes?" Edsen asked.

"They might, but I don't know. *Indira* doesn't belong to Outward-Bound, does she?"

"Jameel said it's a Shivan ferryship. What's a ferry?"

Marianne considered. She knew the word from somewhere. "There's a ferryman called Charon in one of the stories I read. He had a boat, and he used to take dead people across a river called the Styx."

"Did they get buried there?"

"No. It was their spirits he took, to a place called the Underworld. I suppose that means a ferry is a boat that takes people, or their spirits, from one place to another."

"Terra must be a strange place."

"These stories are really old. Centuries old. That's why we've got them."

"Stories about what life's like on Terra *now* would be more useful," Edsen said.

"Not really. We're never going to go there."

CHAPTER EIGHT: INSURANCE

Indira in space– Shivan Year 6 Day 581
Doctor Dorotea Suchet

The burials of the dead of *Elysian Dawn* were by no means completed. The technicians and some of the other *Indira* personnel had worked willingly for the first couple of days, but they were hampered by lack of experience and lack of proper tools, not to speak of the discomfort of doing heavy work in iso-gear. The soil was light and crumbly, but most of them were unaccustomed to digging more than a garden patch. Clearly, the task would take weeks, if not months, and the two Provosts aboard were increasingly restless.

"We can't stay here forever. *Indira* is meant to be servicing the Shiva — Terra run," Rose said.

Dorotea was pretty sure it was not the same Rose who had helped Daffodil Lan in her attempt to save Farne Causeway or, in fact, the same Rose who had piloted the lander. They were all about the same height, and all spoke in clipped, modulated tones, but this one seemed sharper.

"We were authorised to take thirty standard days," she reminded.

"Yes, but that was on the supposition we'd be repatriating these people to Shiva."

"We were sent to help them any way we could," Harry Fejoa corrected, sharply, for him. He stared Rose down, which was difficult to do with someone almost entirely concealed in vibrantly-coloured robes and self-importance.

Dorotea wondered if that was how the ship-born felt about them. The ones who'd spent that ill-fated period aboard *Indira* knew what they looked like, of course, but the older ones couldn't have much idea. She'd seen some of the mid-sized ones peeping through the shuttle view screen, but they wouldn't have known who was who.

As a Terran living long-term on Shiva, she was used to seeing people wearing the full burnous, hood and veil. It was the only way to survive outside the buildings for more than a few minutes. However, she was equally used to seeing them with their hoods back and veils down, at the very least, as soon as they stepped inside, and most of them removed the burnous entirely. The young Citizens, especially, liked to display their jewel-coloured clothing, which showed to great advantage against the salt-white interior walls of the buildings.

They were all so *healthy*, those Citizens. If she'd been working on Terra, her patients would have been far less pride-inducing . . . but probably more interesting.

"Do you have an alternative suggestion?" she asked mildly.

Annoying the Provosts wasn't a good move, if she wanted to keep her comfortable tenure on Shiva. Even after several standard years of residence, she couldn't bring herself to think of the planet as *Mother Shiva*. Indeed, why would she? Surely Shiva was a *male* aspect of a Hindu god? Not that the Shivans were Hindu. Their god, if they had one, was the planet itself.

"We should leave now, and spend the remaining time in quarantine," Rose said, snapping Dorotea back to the present.

"There is merit in that suggestion," Lime decreed.

"I meant, an alternative for helping the ship-born bury their dead."

"Have Outward-Bound fund a new mission. They can bring proper equipment and vital supplies," Rose said.

"Perhaps an autonomous bio-habitat would allow for extended periods of aid," Lime suggested.

The expense of these solutions would be far beyond what any company would be able to pay, especially since Outward-Bound and all its assets now belonged to Shiva. The Provosts undoubtedly knew that. The Provosts undoubtedly didn't care. Presumably, they saw a rescue mission as bringing glory to Mother Shiva, while a mundane burial mission was not to be considered in the same light. Shiva didn't bury its dead Terra-born—it cremated them and returned them to Terra. What Shiva would do with dead Citizens was a mystery. So far, there had never been any.

"Thank you," Dorotea said, and backed away. She did not, could not, and didn't want to understand the Provosts' point of view.

Harry Fejoa and Daffodil Lan visited her in her quarters not long after.

She looked up enquiringly. "Yes?"

"We're leaving," Harry said.

"What? When?"

"Tomorrow afternoon, after we've finished the visual report map." He must have seen her objection because he held up a hand. "Simple maths tells us we can't possibly finish the burial detail in the remaining time, and we have no say in the matter."

"Who has? The captain?" Dorotea asked.

"No, he's an employee like the rest of us. Guess."

"I suppose Citizen Singh might—"

Harry shook his head. "This hasn't been the best experience for young Meera."

Dorotea shied back reflexively. She knew, objectively, that Citizen Meera Singh was simply a glossy, intelligent, imperious teenager, like the others of her generation, but she'd had enough years on Shiva to react as programmed. "What do you know about Citizen Singh?" she asked a trifle stiffly.

"Not a lot. I have met her, though."

"But you're based on Terra. I know you came for the conference, but Citizen Singh wasn't there."

"This wasn't my first visit. I was seconded to Krishna a couple of standard years ago."

"I didn't know that."

"Why should you?"

"The population is still low enough for me to be aware of new appointments in medical circles. I ought to have known."

"I was officially unofficial . . . you might say, undercover. It's easy enough to pass unrecognised with the burnous," Harry said.

"But what was the point?"

"I was brought in, along with a couple of other Terrans, to observe the young Citizens, psychologically speaking. I reported directly to the Provosts, and I have no idea whether they took notice of my report or not."

"Was it a favourable report?" Daffodil ventured. Dorotea saw she was staring at Harry Fejoa as if he'd sprouted antlers.

"Not especially. Oh, she is normal enough — for a person brought up in such an abnormal situation. I'd say that basically, she's an intelligent and sociable young woman. Unfortunately, she's also dictatorial, rash and has an inflated sense of her own intelligence."

"She *is* intelligent."

"Oh, she certainly is, and she's had every possible chance to develop that intelligence. However, her judgement and ability to see ramifications from her actions are no better than her brother's, and we know what happened to him."

"I thought you liked Ambassador Singh," Daffodil said.

"I did, very much. He was a likable person, considering the way he was treated. Think of being brought up with every advantage and then discovering you were no more than a rehearsal, or maybe a guinea pig!

"I only wish I'd known he was making that first descent with the comm-set. I'd have cautioned him about iso-gear."

"Apparently, the metallurgist didn't wear it either," Daffodil said.

"No. But then, he'd been working on Juno, and that's atmospherically safe, at least. They have some unlikely wildlife, but none of it has proved dangerous to humans."

"So, you've worked there as well," Dorotea said mildly.

Harry grinned. "As a matter of fact, yes. No exotic diseases, but I was interested in the socio-mental effect of living among utterly foreign surroundings. Historically, humans have always tried to take their surroundings with them, leading to inappropriate clothing, cultural attitudes out of step with the new society, and the introduction of plants and animals that either do poorly or else do entirely too well . . ."

"The ship-born must fascinate you, then," Daffodil said coolly.

"Indeed, but that doesn't preclude me from seeing them as individuals. I thought from the beginning the idea of raising a society with no idea of their ancestry and history was—" He broke off as Daffodil and Dorotea both turned to stare at him. "What?"

"Just how old are you, Doctor Fejoa?" Dorotea asked.

"Guess."

She examined his face, brown, smooth and unwrinkled, and his dark hair. That might be the result of *staycolour*, but to her, it looked natural. She took one of his hands and examined his nails. "Smile," she said.

He did so, and she noted the faint beginning of crows'

feet, invisible until then.

"You'd pass for late-twenties in a kind light, but I'd say you're somewhere between thirty-five and forty, weighted to the lower end," she said.

"Hmm," Harry said.

"Well?"

"It's not a bad guess, but I'm certainly older than you are."

Dorotea inspected him again and said emphatically, "Not a chance. I'm sixty-three."

"Really? You don't look it. I was born in twenty-two-oh-seven, though, so I was four when you were born." He held up a hand when Daffodil exclaimed in disbelief. "You must know *First Launch* wasn't something Outward-Bound thought up one day and then said, *Make it so!* It took seventeen years to build *Elysian Dawn,* and a few years before that to plan the logistics. I worked on her as a very junior medical officer in the early twenty-two thirties.

"Outward-Bound was then considering different methods of making the project work. One of their notions was to have the original group sleep through the trip, settle and then raise families on the planet. That would have meant stas-tanks for the journey, so they asked for volunteers to test the tech. It was off the record, and we all signed contracts and waivers."

"Why would you want to risk it?" Daffodil asked.

Harry said blandly, "Money. Adventure. The honour of being at the vanguard. And of course, the contracts secured our places on board for *First Launch* if we survived. I had no close family, and I knew they'd need medics, so it seemed a good chance. We'd already spent a year in isolation in a simulation, being monitored for psychological ill-effects from being cut off, so this seemed the logical follow-up."

"What happened?" Dorotea asked.

"We entered the stas-tanks for a couple of days, first, then out we came for exhaustive testing. The next round was a few weeks. And so, it went on. Then came the big one—a five-year stretch. Only a couple of us signed up for that. When I came out of that one, even I was surprised at how well I functioned in the immediate aftermath. It's not like being cryogenically frozen. It's just being slowed right down. So, they woke me up, gave me a bit of physiotherapy, and after a good meal and a sleep I rolled up to debrief." He glanced at Daffodil. "Don't bother trying to count up the missing years, Daff. It was over seven by then—eight if you count the year in the sim. I was chronologically thirty-eight, and biologically and culturally thirty. All my brain cells were intact, and I felt fantastically enthusiastic and well-rested.

"I went into that debriefing bulging with confidence, but what I got was a handshake thank-you and the news the tank method had been sidelined, and they'd decided to go for a generation ship approach."

"Why?"

"They never clearly explained, but from what I gathered, it was to do with their earnest wish that the new settlement would carry none of the prejudices and preconceptions of the past. Sending settlers who'd come of age on Terra meant they'd have those deep-seated ideas. Also, they'd have clear memories of Terran life. Despite their devotion to the project, they might decide they wanted to go on with a lifestyle they knew. The idea was that if they knew they'd never be settlers themselves, they'd pass down only useful things to their descendants. That didn't include Terran history, by the way, and of course, there were no books that reflected contemporary Terran life."

"Well, that accounts for the gaps in the ship-borns' knowledge. They have no idea of any form of writing that doesn't involve a pencil. Fortunately, they do understand something of genetics," Dorotea said.

"What happened to the other five-year person?" Daffodil asked.

Harry Fejoa shrugged. "She never woke. Neither did some of the animals they'd tanked for extended periods. As it turned out, tanking *young* animals worked far better, but of course, there was no way they were tanking human kids without their parents. They also ruled out doing families, in case the kids woke up and the parents didn't. That's a bit ironic if you consider the current situation."

"It still doesn't explain you, unless the goop is the Fountain of Youth?" Dorotea said.

"Goop?"

"That's what Edson Balm calls the life-support liquid in the tanks."

"Goop. Good enough. Better than Bio-equality-stasis-sustainability-environmental-fluid, which is what *we* called it. And no, it isn't the Fountain of Youth.

"They'd swept the tank program off the board for humans, but I'd complied with everything they wanted, and so I fully expected to be one of the thousand selected for *First Launch*. A fellow called Chavez explained to me why that wasn't going to happen. *Too old*, he said. I pointed out that I was only thirty, no matter what my birth certificate said, but he said even if I stayed thirty for the next ten years, I'd be too old because they'd decided to go for an upper cut-off of twenty-five for adults and five for children.

"I pointed out that I had a contract, but they pulled the *circumstances beyond our control* clause. I made a nuisance of myself, so they paid me off. It was a good lump sum, and I used it to set up my own tank system."

"Aren't they awfully expensive?" Daffodil asked.

"The initial outlay is, but ongoing costs aren't bad, especially when you consider the money saved on day-to-day living and the effect of compound interest. Anyway, I proved my point by putting in a good few years and emerging in excellent shape, but by then, the bird had flown. FetTL Mark two had made human tanking pretty much irrelevant, although it's still used for cure-coasting. I cut my losses, got some updated accelerated training, checked out Juno and Shiva, and here I am." He turned out his hands. "Obviously, I kept up to date with *First Launch* and the fortunes of Outward-Bound where possible. When this mission came up, it seemed like fate. I jumped at the chance to meet the folk of *Elysian Dawn*." He gave a bitter smile. "I thought maybe my chance had come again . . . I intended to jump ship and stay on the planet for a couple of weeks at least, and then to be a part of whatever they decided to do next. I was sure they'd do *something* interesting. They were a community of adventurers. They were never going to settle quietly back home, or even on Shiva. Only, as it turns out, once again I'm too old to join the game, and this time it's a physical fact and not some damned Outward-Bounder ruling."

Daffodil stared at him, shaking her head slowly. "Would you ever go into the tank again?"

"I will, after this mission. I still have the system, and it's opened up a lot of possibilities. In theory, I could still be around in a hundred years. Tanking is time-travel, but it goes only one way."

Dorotea sighed. "Fascinating though this story has been, we still have the problem of the ship-born. And Harry, you still need to enlarge on your cryptic remark about Citizen Meera Singh. You said, or implied, she's *done herself no good* with this venture. Why? It's not her fault this situation arose."

"I meant just what I said. Taking this as a test case to see if Citizens who have enjoyed accelerated education, material advantage and a bucketful of positive reinforcement, are ready to rule their own destiny and their planet's, then I'd say the answer is pretty conclusive, wouldn't you?"

Dorotea eyed him quizzically. "And you'll be reporting back to the Provosts of Shiva?"

"No need. We have two, or possibly six or eight, of them right here."

"I assume they've already let Outward-Bound and Citizen Singh know the mission has been less than a stellar success."

They were all silent. Dorotea was tired and disappointed, and she supposed young Doctor Lan was, too. She contemplated Harry Fejoa, trying to see the complicated personality underlying that surface affability. She wondered who the other five-year tank sleeper had been. Not a sister. He'd said he had no close family. Maybe a girlfriend or fiancée. That might explain why he'd continued with the tank experiment, effectively distancing himself from her in time. It wouldn't keep him from mourning, but it would effectively stop other people from keeping her memory fresh.

"I suppose if we had a functioning stas-tank system the remainder of the deceased could be put in stasus until we work out how best to help the ship-born," she said.

"There are animal tanks on *Elysian Dawn*," Daffodil pointed out.

"They drained them when they let the animals out. Evidently, they were malfunctioning, anyway. Perhaps the remaining bodies can stay sealed up in the family quarters? We could make one big push tomorrow before we leave."

"That's probably the best idea. That way, part of the ship becomes a mausoleum, while leaving the areas they need to access free from visual reminders," Harry said.

Daffodil shivered, although it wasn't cold. "Are you sure we'll be able to go down again tomorrow? Now that we've been ordered back, we might not be authorised for another drop."

"We'll be authorised," Dorotea said, a bit grimly.

"Oh?" Harry raised one eyebrow.

"Poor Ambassador Singh has one last role to play. He's sealed up in stasi-sheet in the medical room, if you remember. We still have to take him down to the surface."

"I thought he'd been taken with the children we lost," Daffodil said, frowning.

"No. I had a feeling something like this might be pulled, and he is our insurance. I promised the ship-born some printed documents. I've been steadily amassing those, and I had to make sure I got to deliver them."

"The Provosts won't be pleased," Harry said.

Dorotea gave a faint malicious smile. "I know."

Chapter Nine: Unfixable

Indira in space– Shivan Year 6 Day 582
Doctor Harry Fejoa

Harry helped Dorotea Suchet round up as many willing, and several unwilling, able-bodied helpers as possible for her final visit to the surface. They packed the huge wad of print-out in a stasi-sheet. It wasn't real paper, but the same film used for the *peel-the-pear* map of the planet, thin, flexible and translucent until laid on a firm surface. It was nearly indestructible, so it was used only when permanence was required.

Harry added a copy of the map, now updated from the one Passim Dee had taken. No one knew what had happened to that, and although it might show up when someone located the metallurgist's body, the new one had a good deal more detail. He'd had Dov Talman scan for Dee's comm-set, but the scan had come up empty.

They arrived at the shuttle-hutch to find a group of techs clustered around the lander, trying to repair the land-legs. Sidestepping them, they entered the first shuttle and Harry moved to the controls.

"What about the ambassador?"

"Next trip," Dorotea said serenely.

Harry tilted his head in amused admiration. "You're really milking it, Dorotea. You realise this will probably get you expelled from Shiva?"

"I expect so, but what can they do to me, really? I don't

think they'll abandon me on the planet since that would mean abandoning their shuttle, too. And what about you?"

"You forget, I'm not tied to Shiva. The tank awaits." He smiled at Dorotea. He'd never married or been in a serious relationship since Rachel, but it occurred to him that if he'd met a woman like Dorotea, he might have stayed out of the tank and settled in the present instead of reaching for the future. Too late now. No doubt Dorotea was happily settled with whatever her domestic arrangements might be. In any case, his cultural and biological ages were too far out of synch for him to make a decent partner for any woman, or man, who had not been through the same process.

Rachel. Forever twenty-eight. She wasn't dead. It was just convenient to think of her that way. She was alive, hovering in a tank back on Terra. Did she dream? Why hadn't she woken when they pulled her out? There was no brain damage, nothing to say she wouldn't open her eyes and ask about breakfast. She just hadn't.

Officially, she was dead. Unofficially, she was cure-coasting ... stored until the medical advances could bring her back into wakefulness. She could have been kept alive with tubes and a special bed, but she'd have aged her youth away while she waited. There was another reason, too.

He didn't like to spend too long out of the tank himself. When she woke, he wanted to be recognisable as the man she knew. After this trip, he'd go back in for another decade or so. Maybe they could wake together.

He cross-checked the shuttle and gave the order for iso-gear to be sealed, and then he threw the lever to release the clamps from the cradle. The shuttle swung free, but although the motor powered up, it sounded odd, giving a vibration that set Harry's teeth on edge. He powered down.

"What's wrong with it?" Dorotea asked.

"I don't know. Better ask the techs to have a look."

"I'd rather not attract more attention than we need."

"Want to take the other one instead?"

"Might be best."

Harry tried to get the shuttle back into its cradle, but it was sluggish. When he finally succeeded, he was scowling. He wasn't risk-averse, but he thought taking a malfunctioning shuttle down to a planet that could kill him was a risk too far, even for him.

He left that shuttle, and strolled towards the second one, only to be stopped by one of the techs, the one whose name tag proclaimed him as Terrence *Terror* Australis. "You can't take that one out, Doc."

"Looks as if we'll have to. The other one's running rough."

"This bastard's not running at all." The tech jerked his head at the second shuttle.

Harry had a bad feeling about this. "What's wrong with it?"

"If we knew that, mate, we'd have fixed it." Australis huffed out a spurt of anger and then said more moderately, "Sorry, Doc, but this is one helluva jinxed trip if you ask me. I'm sorry about those kids stuck down there on that cursed planet, especially the ones that died on this ship, but it's been one damned thing after another. We've lost two passengers, including a Citizen's brother, those Provosts are giving us curry, and now we're being asked to fix the unfixable."

"What do you mean by unfixable?" Harry asked.

"What do you think I mean? Un-bloody-fixable! Never meant to be fixed. This tech doesn't break down. The twinning is just to speed up disembarkation when we don't land the whole ship."

"It must be fixable though," Harry argued.

Australis gave him a straight stare. "Look, Doc. If you

find a bloke with his head cut off, do you try and fix him?"

"No."

"Why don't you?"

"Because he's dead."

"See? He's unfixable. You can stitch the head back on, but that's just cosmetic. He's not fixed. That's the way this shuttle is. It needs a new nuclear battery, but it was assembled around the battery. You don't change that battery over the way you do with a torch. You make a new bloody shuttle around a new battery. Get it?"

Harry got it. What he didn't get was what to do about it. He had a feeling of being backed into a corner, and he didn't like it. Either the tech was right, and this mission was jinxed, or else someone, somewhere, was trading on the idea of a jinx.

He returned to the first shuttle, and Dorotea looked at him expectantly.

"How likely is it that someone—the Provosts, for example—would sabotage two shuttles to prevent this last trip down?" he asked her.

Dorotea looked honestly surprised. "Why would they? They're agitating to abort the mission, but a few hours won't make a difference, and we've been down before."

"I know. It doesn't make sense to me, either. The only ones with any motive for sabotage would be Outward-Bound, supposing they made some error that led to this whole disaster. Or . . . I suppose they *might* be holding to the whole *keep 'em ignorant* ruling. But it can't be them either. It was Outward-Bound that arranged for the rescue."

"It really wasn't us, either," one of the volunteers quietly said.

Harry and Dorotea turned to look at her. Like them, she wore an iso-suit, so she was anonymous in face and form. Her voice was soft, and distorted by the isolation field, but she seemed of average height and might be middle-aged.

Harry frowned.

"I think that's Rose. Well, one of the Roses," Dorotea said. She turned to the person in the suit. "You're the Rose who helped Daffodil Lan with Farne Causeway, aren't you?"

The person made no reaction for a moment, and then she said, "Never mind who I am, Doctor Suchet. Just take it as fact that no Provost would commit sabotage of this sort. This is a Shivan ship. It's not in Mother Shiva's best interests to have any part of *Indira* seen to fail."

"I see. That leaves *actual* equipment failure. We'll have to take this one after all." Harry felt a lurch of unease at the thought, but he returned to the controls. "Before I start again, I suggest you all think about whether you want to risk it. If not, you'd better leave this shuttle now. I think we'll get down, but I can't guarantee a safe return."

Seven of the more reluctant volunteers moved quietly out of the shuttle. Harry didn't blame them.

"Anyone else?"

Another two edged towards the door.

"Rose?"

"My name's not Rose."

Maybe not *now*. "What do we call you then, supposing you're coming with us?"

"Kat will do. Kat with a K."

Harry closed up and swung the shuttle out of the cradle. It jerked part way, shuddered, and balked.

"Dammit!" Harry swivelled the lever, which worked on a ball-and-socket joint and which should have tilted smoothly. Instead, it ground and stuck. He tried to shift it, but this time it froze as if it had gravel in the joint or had cross-threaded.

"I think that's that, Dorotea. You'll have to call Edsen and tell him we're not able to come."

"I promised them this print-out," Dorotea protested.

"I know. But I think it's going to have to wait for the next swing-by by another ship. Or you can send it via comm-set. Call him."

Dorotea took a comm-set out of her pouch and touched the screen.

"Please state your name and required contact."

"Doctor Dorotea Suchet. I require contact with com-tat Edsen Balm of Elydia."

"Ed — re — ing." The reply stuttered.

Dorotea tapped the screen and tried again. "Edsen, our shuttles are malfunctioning. We can't come down. Will send material via comm-set. Repeat, shuttles malfunctioning. We can't come down. Will send material via comm-set."

She paused, but only broken syllables responded.

Dorotea held up the comm-set. For a moment, Harry thought she was going to slam it onto the floor of the unresponsive shuttle, but she just thrust it back into her pouch.

There was a chill silence for a few seconds, and then she said, "It's that *damned* planet. It's got to be. First of all, it brought down *Elysian Dawn* and gradually killed its systems and a lot of its people. Then it went for the comm-set, the lander, and now it's murdered the shuttles."

Harry's feeling of impending doom settled into a cold lump in his chest. Walking stiffly, he left the shuttle again and approached Terrence Australis, the tech who'd intercepted him before. "I know you said these things are unfixable, but I suggest you check them for anything that shouldn't be present, right now."

"Eh? Like what?" Australis asked.

"That silver substance from the planet."

"They were purged. Not a flea's chance of surviving Dingo Soap," the tech reminded him.

"Yes, but did you check the *outside* works . . ."

"Oh, shit!" Australis snapped into action, and Harry

knew things were going to get very bad, very soon.

CHAPTER TEN: TEARS FROM THE SKY

Elydia 17 01 01
Marianne Arcadia

The helpers from *Indira* had assisted with removing more stores from *Elysian Dawn,* using the exit through which they'd released the animals. All the lost ones not already in the ground were wrapped in stasi-sheets which, the techs said, could serve as permanent shrouds.

Marianne had lost count of the days since it all began. Sometimes, it seemed a year or more, and at others, she woke with thoughts of Jeremiah or her parents and what they might do today.

She tried to keep herself firmly in the present. This was the way life was, and the way it was going to be. The old dreams were gone. New dreams lay ahead.

At least it was never dull.

One night, she heard something strange outside the shelter.

Jameel Singh had warned Edsen about Elydian animals. Could it be them? It wasn't the goats, sheep or horses, who tended to be quiet at night. It certainly wasn't the chicks, which slept in feathery bundles in one of the shelters.

She emerged from the shelter and stopped dead in astonishment.

Drops of water were falling from the sky. The stars and three moons, usually brilliant silver and white in the night, were gone.

Could this be rain? In the gardens of *Elysian Dawn,* they'd sprinkled water on the plants in a simulation of naturally-occurring rain. Jeremiah had spoken of it. And here was the real thing.

Needing to share the wonder of it, she called softly, "Ed? Are you awake in there?"

Edsen came out of the next shelter almost right away, and she heard his startled exclamation. "What the flid is that!"

"Rain, I think." She tilted her face and opened her mouth to taste the drops. "Yes, just water."

"Rain!" He reached out to touch her cheek. "You're smiling. What are you smiling about, Mim?"

"Rain! Real rain! I have to smile. It's better than crying."

"I suppose so."

Jeremiah, bearing Rain as a family name himself, would have made some poetic or romantic quip about *tears from the sky,* at that point, but Edsen wasn't made that way. Marianne was glad. She put her arm around him. It was something she did from time to time because he was so alone.

She often got hugs from Bede and the two little Rain children, and Aleph sometimes sat down and leaned against her, especially when he remembered his friend Farne and grieved for him. Sherry and Panji often hugged her, too, but she'd noticed the Top-Ender boys stood apart from everyone but little ones. But . . . perhaps they always had. She couldn't remember seeing Carolina hugging Ed the way Anya had still hugged Aleph and Bede.

She remembered one of Moon's matter-of-fact talks during a routine gauging when she was fifteen.

"We all need touch, Marianne. Don't be afraid of that outside your family. Just make sure the other person knows what you're offering, what you want to give, and why. Do you understand?"

She'd nodded doubtfully.

Moon had grinned at her. "You will. And don't forget, boys need it, too. Just now and then, you might need to remind them a hug is sometimes only a hug and not an open invitation to start making babies. Do you understand *that*?"

Now, in the rain, she put her other arm around Edsen in a proper hug. "Don't take this wrong," she said.

He gave her a friendly squeeze and kissed her cheek. "I won't."

The excitement of actual rain warmed her for a little, and so did contact with someone else's body. Soon, though, she realised her back was getting cold. It was time for the hug to end. "Come on, Ed, we'd better get back inside. Change your shirt for a dry one, or you'll make the blankets wet."

"Yes, Mim. What's that noise?" Edsen said. He stepped away from her, and her front turned cold as well.

Marianne listened. "It sounds like the ducklings . . . I hope they're all right."

"I expect so. Flid! I wonder if that means they *like* this rain!"

"Why not? They like water." She shivered and moved inside.

Bede, Inga and Franz were still asleep, and Sherry, who had no family left, was cuddled up with Amrita. Where was Aleph? Marianne sighed. He'd probably decided to sleep in another shelter with some of the other Elves. Or maybe he was with Tamma Windward and her little brothers who shared a shelter with the Moon blossoms. He would be all right. Farne was dead, but then, he'd chosen to leave Elydia anyway, and Aleph had chosen to stay.

The sound of the rain pattered on the shelters all night, and well into the morning. When it finally stopped, Marianne emerged and found Edsen, Grant and Bede staring expectantly at the sky. It was grey and seemed close to the ground. Presumably, that was to do with the rain.

"Have you talked to Doctor Suchet yet?" she asked.

"She tried, I think, but . . ." Edsen held up the comm-set.

It seemed lopsided. "Have you unscrewed that one, too, Bede?" Marianne asked.

Bede grinned at her. He looked unrepentant. "Yes, I did. Edsen said I could."

"Ed!"

Edsen gave her a half smile and shrugged.

Bede went on, "Guess what, Mim? It's got silver stuff in it like the old one. And guess what again?"

"What?" she asked, tweaking his ear.

"We unscrewed it before, while it was still working and there wasn't any silver stuff in it, then. It must be the silver that makes it stop working."

The silvering had almost stopped *her* working, but she didn't remind him of that.

Unlike Edsen and Aleph, Bede wore his hair cropped short, and she noticed it seemed to be changing colour at the roots.

More silvering, no doubt. She reached out and rubbed her hand over it. To her relief, it still felt like hair, but then, their changing skin still felt just like skin.

"Do you think the shuttle can come down with all that grey up there in the sky?" she asked instead.

"Pretty sure it can."

Marianne hoped so. She wanted to ask Doctor Suchet if rain was likely to happen often.

After a while, she got tired of waiting, and she and Sherry went into *Elysian Dawn* to sort through more books, and to make sure the stores had not got wet.

Something seemed to be troubling Sherry, and Marianne finally asked her what it was.

"I dreamed about Pip, only she was older, and when I woke up Amrita was with me, and I thought for a second it *was* Pip," Sherry said.

Marianne understood. Pip was Sherry's baby sister. She had died with their parents in the crash. No wonder Sherry dreamed of her. Marianne sometimes dreamed of Jeremiah, Anya, Markus and her pretty cousins. Old dreams. Now she needed new ones.

She wished Olivia and Mia could have lived. Two more Top-Ender girls would have been handy. They'd been fun, in their slightly intimidating way. They'd been family.

Sherry continued, breaking into her thoughts. "I know we said we'd leave the lost ones in the family quarters where they are, but I feel so bad for Pip. She never had a chance to see the sky, or . . ." Sherry's words trailed off, and she started to weep silently. "My parents saw sky on Terra, and I'm seeing it on Elydia."

"You'd like to bring them out under the sky?"

Sherry nodded, her shoulders shaking. "C-can't manage them without help, but Pip's only so little—"

Marianne hated the thought of entering the family quarters, but Sherry's distress moved her. Jeremiah now lay in the soil of Elydia, his resting place marked by some silver stones she'd laid out in a ring.

All the lost ones in the soil had stones in different patterns. Hillman Hope, a Top-Ender with two sisters among the Elves and a toddler brother, was keeping a record of the markers as well as transcribing the notes he'd made with Doctor Suchet. He was just as methodical as Momo.

Anya and Markus were still in their quarters, and Marianne thought they wouldn't mind being there. At least they were together, in the place they'd expected to live for the rest of their days. One day, maybe, she could make them markers. They might even find a way to write the lost names on the sides of *Elysian Dawn*.

She put her arm around Sherry. "Let's go and get Pip and

bring her out in her stasi-sheet."

She wasn't too sure about the stasi-sheets, but she knew the folk from *Indira* had said they were necessary to keep the bodies recognisable. Without these, they'd go all out of shape the way plants did when they were kept out of the soil for too long. That was called *decay*, Doctor Benz had said. He'd come to the surface only once, but he'd told the older kids some things they needed to know about death and bodies.

He'd told them death was nothing to be afraid of. It was something that happened to everyone. When people died in years to come, they should get them snug in the ground within three days. He'd even taught them some words to say as a gentle goodbye.

Ashes to ashes and dust to dust and our love to warm your dreams.

They scrambled to the family quarters. With a shiver, Marianne cracked open the door to the Cliffside apartment. Was it imagination, or was *Elysian Dawn* still settling under her own weight? How much longer could they safely enter their old home?

Inside was a jumble, but someone, presumably one of the Terran techs, had picked up the sling crib from where it would have fallen and balanced it back on its pegs, next to the long shapes of Sherry's parents. It hung lopsided, and inside, wrapped in a stasi-sheet, was a small bundle that must be Pip. Marianne bent and lifted it gently.

Sherry was sobbing, and Marianne felt tears coursing down her cheeks in response. "I'll bring her. You lead the way and find a place for her to rest. Maybe near the other babies," she said.

As they crept along the wall-turned-floor, this seemed even less of a good idea. It wasn't only Sherry's distress that troubled Marianne, but the knowledge that the same scene could be played over many times as the thoughts of others turned to people they'd lost. It made sense to want them safe in the ground, especially to those who'd heard Doctor Benz's matter-of-fact lecture. On the other hand, was it worth the possible loss of the living if the ship cracked and settled again?

They came to the exit, and Sherry stepped into the soft grey light which today replaced the usual brilliance of day-light on Elydia.

"Over here," she said, indicating a spot not far from the exit, just to the side of a hump of the silver rock. Marianne saw the earth had already been dug out. It was damp from the rain, with specks of glittering silver.

Sherry must have been planning this for a while.

"We'll leave her in the stasi-sheet," she said.

Sherry shook her head vehemently. "I want her to be under the sky, just for a little bit."

"Sherry, you know she won't look the way she did. You remember what Doctor Benz told us. She might be all . . . um . . ."

Sherry held out her arms. "I don't mind. She's my sister."

Numbly, Marianne handed over the so-small bundle. Sherry laid it down on the wet grass, and tenderly unwrapped it. Marianne shut her eyes, not wanting to see what might have happened to a baby many days dead.

She heard a gasp from Sherry, and her eyes snapped open. "What is it?"

For just a second, she thought, hoped, the little girl was miraculously alive. Of course, she wasn't, and yet what she saw was almost as surprising.

Pip Cliffside would never walk the surface of Elydia, would never feel the rain, or giggle at the ducklings. She'd never grow up as an Elydian girl, to learn to touch and to love and to find out what to say. There were many things she would never do, but Marianne saw she was part of Elydia, even so. She lay in her little day-gown, dusted in silver.

"She's like us," Sherry said softly. She brushed her tiny sister's cheek, her tears dropping like the rain in the night. "Why did Doctor Benz tell us she'd go all squishy? She's *beautiful.*"

Marianne managed to smile. "He might know a lot about how things work on Terra. He doesn't know much about how they work on Elydia."

Chapter Eleven: A Promise Kept

Elydia 17 01 01
Edsen Balm

Edsen was disappointed that his comm-set had failed again. It looked as if Elydia was determined her new population was going to be cut off from *Indira,* Krishna Tower two and thus, Outward-Bound.

He didn't care much about *Indira,* and he felt awkward about speaking with Citizen Meera Singh after his new home had claimed her brother. He did regret losing touch with Cornelia Conti, but he hoped the folk on *Indira* would thank her for what she had tried to do.

The shuttle didn't come.

Evening started to fall, and people gradually stopped peering into the sky. The greyness had cleared, and the light shone down again, just in time for Caspar to slide beyond the horizon. Edsen knew it wasn't really Caspar doing the sliding, but Elydia turning its back on the light. *Elysian Dawn* had maintained artificial days, to keep plants and people in normal rhythm. Elydia did it naturally.

Edsen had given a lot of thought to Marianne's suggestion that the Top-Ender boys should pool their knowledge to pass on to the younger ones. It still felt strange to be an older person, but he supposed he'd get used to it. It was bound to be embarrassing, trying to educate the Elves, so he'd decided on a broader approach.

If information on how boys became men could be slipped

in with other things, it would be easier. The Elves needed schooling, anyway, and it was up to the older ones to provide it.

Edsen's new goal was to write down as much as he could about all the things he knew.

He'd start with what he'd learned from being a com-tat and move on from there.

As the dark came on, he moved away from the lights of the shelters and tried to visualise the Celestial map, the way it had been just before the crash. If he could copy that down, he could teach the younger kids about where they were in space. He and Marianne had found the ones his parents and the Colliers had made, but they were disappointingly rough. He lay back with his arms folded behind his head and looked up at the sky. The stars were appearing, and one moon showed above the horizon. They hadn't named the three moons yet. Maybe they should. Maybe they should name lots of things. Marianne had made a start with wool-wood, kissing-fruit, and pondcups. The names she thought up were nice to say, easy to remember and pleasant to picture, just like her.

His mind was wandering among the stars and inventing his future when he saw a jagged streak of brightness in the sky. A comet? A meteor? He went through the Celestial bodies Eduard and Carolina had taught him.

Whatever it was, it was coming to land. He hoped it wasn't *Indira,* falling out of the sky as *Elysian Dawn* had done.

Flid! It was coming fast. He got up, staring away into the night as if he could pierce the blackness.

The bright orange faded and the thing, whatever it was, fell the rest of the way to invisibility. Edsen felt a vibration through the ground.

It had landed.

He looked back at the shelters, his first impulse to go and get Marianne.

No. He'd do this alone, in case it was *Indira*. The people would be dead, if not now, in a few days. He knew there was nothing to do to help them. Doctor Suchet had told them so. Once the racking began, you either got better quite quickly, or you died.

Flid! Hadn't there been enough dying already?

Slowly, reluctantly, Edsen walked away into the dark.

He'd been walking for more than a couple of hours, he thought. His feet were reminding him it was farther and longer than he'd walked in a while. The grass was interspersed with woolwood groves, and he hoped he could find his way back. Still, *Elysian Dawn* was huge. She should be visible from a long way off, especially when Caspar rose over the horizon.

The second moon came up with the third on its heels, and he rested for a while, ate some kissing-fruit from a bush and drank from pondcup leaves. He smelled something savoury and different, and he tracked it down to a mass of soft domes growing directly in the grass.

Mushrooms? They had mushrooms in the gardens on the ship. Carolina usually cooked them, but they could be eaten raw. He lifted one free of its stubby stalk. It shone pale in the moons' light, so he tried Marianne's method of rubbing it between finger and thumb and dabbing the juice on his tongue.

It seemed safe, so he took a cautious bite. The texture was different from the fruit they'd been eating, chewy and satisfying. It tasted more than pleasant. Edsen looked down as he chewed, noting with pleasure the large colony of the things. They probably weren't mushrooms, but they could be just as good. He ate it all and bent to pick another.

He was contemplating taking some back to the shelters when he heard a faint sound away to his left. It rose and fell, stopped, and was answered. It sounded busy and purposeful.

Excitement rose in Edsen, along with expectation. Jameel had mentioned Elydian animals. He'd stressed that some could be dangerous, but this sound didn't suggest danger to Edsen. It was just as cheery as the sound the ducks had made when celebrating the rain.

Something moved on the periphery of his vision, travelling low to the ground, scurrying like the ducklings as they headed for the pool. These moved faster, though, and had more legs and a much wider repertoire of sound.

Edsen's eyes had adjusted to the light from the moons, and he could focus on the hurrying things. They were small, barely topping his ankles. He couldn't tell their colour, but he supposed they were brownish silver. They bustled around him and stopped. The chittering changed to a different sound, and Edsen realised they were eating the mushrooms.

He stayed where he was, not wanting to startle them or to crush them underfoot. He stood ankle deep in the warm and moving mass, entranced, but eventually, he *had* to move. Slowly, he folded his legs, cleared a patch with a gentle sweep of his hand and sat down. The munching stopped abruptly, and one of the creatures made a different sound. It fell on Edsen's ears almost like a word.

"*Heymsss!*" he said, trying to copy it. "Hey-muss."

The merry chittering and munching resumed. The hey-muss, as he thought of them, had accepted him as something that didn't threaten them.

It was nearly dawn when they bustled off, and Edsen noted with some regret that they'd eaten all the mushrooms.

Well, that was a good thing, surely. If he saw them again, he'd watch to see what they ate and see if they would share it.

He got up and walked on, seeing more and different trees as he went, and watching the ground in case of more mushrooms or more of the small Elydian animals. He turned now and then and peered back. Yes, there was *Elysian Dawn*, looming against the lightening sky.

And there, as he turned back, he saw something moving in the near distance.

It was one of the Terrans—he couldn't tell which—clad in an iso-suit.

"Hello?" he called and waved his arms.

The figure oriented on him and came on slowly. Edsen moved to meet him, or her. "Hello?" he said again.

"Hello, Edsen." He recognised the slightly muffled voice.

"Doctor Suchet. Are you all right? What happened? Did *Indira* crash?"

"*Indira* is okay. She's heading home to Shiva."

"But you can't stay here." He was blankly appalled.

"I'm going to have to, but it's all right." She seemed to be looking about and indicated *Elysian Dawn*. "There she is. I was afraid I'd landed too far away to find you. Edsen, I take it your new comm-set has given out?"

He tilted his head, trying to read her mood. "Yes. The silvering is inside it. We think that's what stops it working. I don't see any point in you giving me another one, but please, can you let Cornelia Conti know—"

"You can let her know yourself." Doctor Suchet handed him a comm-set from her pouch.

"I can't talk to her on this."

"Yes, you can, but you should do it quickly because this one probably won't last long either. Harry Fejoa has arranged for Outward-Bound to have a comm-set and with luck, it's already been delivered to their office. Call her now."

"Is Doctor Fejoa with you?"

"No. It's only me, this time. Call Outward-Bound now, and then come back to the lander with me. I've brought you the information I promised, and we have a lot to talk about."

Edsen raised the comm-set and touched the screen.

"Please state your name and required contact."

He drew a deep breath. "Comm-set *Keeper* Edsen Balm from *Elydia*. I require contact with Cornelia Conti, Outward-Bound on Terra."

There was a long silence, and then a face he'd never seen before swam into being on the screen.

The woman had grey hair, and she looked tired and — old. She was older than any person he'd ever seen. Her lips moved, and the silence stretched, and then her voice came in.

"Edsen Balm! I'm so *glad* to hear from you!"

Chapter Twelve: The Request

Outward-Bound Office. May 10th, 2273
Cornelia Conti

The new Shivan-style comm-set was hand-delivered by a
Provost, which was startling. Cornelia had never met
one of those enigmatic cloaked figures before, and she
hadn't even known they came to Terra.

The flowing gown hid the shape beneath, but the strong
turquoise colour must have drawn attention in the streets.
The Outward-Bound office was several storeys up, but Cornelia half-expected a row of fascinated faces looming up beyond the window.

"Hello?" she ventured.

She heard a door creak and realised Woo and Ash must
have been alerted to their visitor.

"Cornelia Conti?"

"Yes. How did you know?"

"I was told you had grey hair," the Provost said.

Of course.

"Have you come to take possession of the office for the
Shivans?" It seemed likely.

"No. I was directed to bring you this." Out of the turquoise robes came a gloved hand, bearing a small black device. It looked like a rather large personal communicator, of
a sort everyone had.

"I have one," Cornelia said politely.

"This comm-set is for interstellar communication. You are

to use it *only* to receive communications from similar models. Is that clear, Director Conti?"

"I suppose—who are you?"

"Call me Turquoise. Someone may contact you—or not. You are not to make any calls yourself."

The veiled Provost turned from the door and walked away.

Cornelia and the others rushed to the window to peer down at the exit of the building. There were several, but only one that led from their quadrant.

They waited, but although they saw several people come and go, none was the turquoise Provost.

Woo accessed the SeeMe that noted everyone entering the building. It was a standard security procedure on Terran high-rises. She ran the visual back an hour, but no flash of distinctive colour showed on screen, and no discreet alarm flashed for danger.

"I suppose she—or he—could have bundled those robes up in a bag, and just stepped in and out in street clothes. The robes might even be reversible, so they could double as a plain dark coat," Woo ventured.

"But *why* the masquerade?"

Woo shrugged. "Who knows? I wonder if this thing will let us get a direct message from *Indira*."

"That would make sense," Tomas Ash said.

"But why would a Provost facilitate that? Bouncing messages from Krishna two and keeping us out of the direct loop lets them control the situation. Why would they give up control? It's not what Shivans do."

Ash said, "Are we even sure it *was* a Provost?"

Their speculation ended as the screen rippled and a face appeared. It was a handsome youngish man with brown hair and a friendly smile. He spoke, and after a pause, his words came through. "*Indira* calling. I'm Harry Fejoa. You three will be Directors Cornelia Conti, Tomas Ash, and Samantha Woo. We've met before, but I don't expect you remember me?"

There was the slightest question in his voice.

Cornelia fought to access a memory from more than two decades in the past. The name *Harry Fejoa* did ring a distant bell. She remembered asking if it was spelled the same way as the fruit and then feeling silly because he must have been asked that so often before.

Samantha Woo nudged her, eyes wide. "It can't be him, but he's the dead spit of a bloke who applied for *First Launch*. We were on that selection committee, remember? Before we became the *faceless ones*."

"Tank man." The nickname came, unbidden, and aloud.

Evidently, Harry Fejoa could read lips, because he laughed almost immediately before the sound could have reached him. "Fair enough, Cornelia. I'm sure you're not the first person to think of me like that."

"You can't be the same person," Woo protested.

"I am. I was still physically thirty when Outward-Bound paid me off. I did make a nuisance of myself back then. Since that time, I've spent more years tanked than any man alive, or dead, for that matter. As a result, I've rather lost track of you all, though I believe Landon Chavez is dead? I didn't like him, but I have nothing against you three. Can you tell me how many others are currently on the board of Outward-Bound?"

Cornelia blinked. "Just us."

"And you still run the company? You've not retired?"

"Technically . . . we were shareholders, but the company now belongs to Shiva. We expect to hand over formally as soon as our current project winds up."

Tomas Ash leaned forward. "If you're on *Indira*, you must know more than we do about the rescue project."

"Well spotted," Fejoa said dryly.

"And you'll know the *Elysian Dawn* voyage has come to a premature ending."

Cornelia said, "Why did you send us this comm-set? Where did you get it? I assume it *was* you?"

Harry Fejoa shook his head, visibly *tsking*. "I didn't set this up to gloat, Cornelia. It hurt when I was booted off the project, especially after—" He broke off, but continued almost immediately. "It's all water under the bridge now. After all, I'd be dead now if I'd made the cut. I'm sorry the project failed. I don't pretend to think your company handled it well, but it was a bold attempt.

"I know you haven't been able to speak directly with any of the *Elysian Dawn* people since their Terra-tat went down, and that's why I arranged the comm-set for you. As you know, our rescue attempt failed quite spectacularly, but I think the remaining children have a good chance of making a successful community on the lines you intended. A boy named Edsen Balm has been given a comm-set, too, and I know he is anxious to contact you. Understand, this is temporary. The comm-set you have will last for the foreseeable future, but planetary conditions where he is mean this may be your only chance to speak with him. I trust you'll make the most of it and not distress him with apologies and regrets."

Cornelia had a hundred questions for this man, and she was sure the others did, too. Remorse, justifications, apologies and pleas trembled to be voiced, but before she, or either of the others, could do so, Harry Fejoa favoured them with his friendly smile, and said, "*Tank Man out.*"

Cornelia put her head in her hands. "I'm too old for this," she said and groaned.

"I know how you feel. This was never meant to happen in our tenure," Woo said.

"It was never meant to happen at all," Ash said sadly.

"To look on the bright side, you can cancel those arrangements for rehoming hundreds of orphaned ship-born," Woo said.

Cornelia, who hadn't even begun arrangements before they became unnecessary, sighed. "It's all been a terrible mess, but in a few days, it'll be over, and we'll never have to stand another watch again."

She felt curiously bereft at the thought. Until that fateful *mayday* call, the long watch had been a habit, a ritual, a keeping-of-faith. It had also—she acknowledged, if only to herself—been a way of sidestepping life. She might as well have spent the last eighteen years in a tank.

"I wonder who will take official charge of the company when this is over," Ash said into the silence.

"I assumed it would be Citizen Singh, but since her brother was a casualty of the mission, she might not want anything to do with it," Cornelia said. She felt sorry Jameel Singh had died. She hadn't known him, but any loss of life was to be deplored, and Outward-Bound was responsible for this debacle.

"I wonder how Tank Man got mixed up with *Indira*," she said.

"Tank Man. You know, I'd forgotten him," Woo mused.

"His girlfriend died . . . he survived, and Chavez didn't give him time to grieve before he hit him with the news that he was no longer eligible for the cut. God! When you look back, we were just so arrogant. We thought we were lords of the cosmos," Ash said, with a sudden rush of emotion.

"*First Launch* and hang the consequences," Woo said.

"Yes, and Chavez died without facing them. I wonder if we need to contact his heir to explain it's all over?"

"She's a child."

"So are what's left of *Elydian Dawn*."

"Lyrica Chavez is in no way to blame for this. She wasn't even born at the time. I think we can let the poor kid remain in happy ignorance, at least until she comes of age," Ash said. He added thoughtfully, "I wish *I* could have remained in happy ignorance."

He and Woo turned bland stares on Cornelia.

"Okay, so it's my fault you didn't, but at least it allowed us to fulfil our promise to be there for journey's end." Cornelia was about to suggest some denatured coffee when the comm-set came to life. She peered into it, expecting to see Harry Fejoa again. Instead, she saw a very strange young man. He had floppy hair, a stubborn face with remarkable grey-silver eyes and skin that glowed in an unearthly way. He looked like a grumpy angel.

"Comm-set *Keeper* Edsen Balm of Elydia for Director Cornelia Conti of Outward-Bound," the voiceover announced.

Cornelia felt a miraculous lift of her spirits. She leaned forward, smiling, and said, "Edsen Balm! I'm so *glad* to hear from you!"

The boy's solemn face relaxed into a charming smile. "It's good to hear from you, too, Director Conti. I want to thank you for answering my father's call. He never expected it."

"I'm afraid it didn't do you any good in the end."

"It let Eduard and Moon and the others know someone cared and that someone was coming to help us. Are there other people from Outward-Bound there?"

"Yes!" Cornelia adjusted the screen, so Woo and Ash could be seen. They introduced themselves.

Edsen met the gaze of each in turn. "Thanks to all of you. I won't be able to talk to you again because Elydia messes up tech. I—we all—want you to know we're all right. Most of the animals came out of the tanks safely. Doctor Suchet has some papers for us to teach us how to look after the animals and how to do things we don't know. We're all looking after the little ones who don't have anyone else."

He paused and looked at them expectantly.

"Is there anything we can do for you?" Cornelia asked, though she didn't see what they could possibly do for the *First Launch* orphans.

"There is one thing we need. I don't know if it's possible, but Momo, who's our healer, says we need more people so we can be a viable colony and not mess up our genes. We—I mean, I, though I expect the others will agree, think there is one possible way to get them. If you ever hear of any children who have lost their families and have nowhere else to go . . . could you send them to live with us? We think anyone under twelve will be all right, though we can't manage babies who aren't weaned. I promise you, we will welcome them, and we'll be good to them. This is a nice planet . . . if it doesn't kill you."

Cornelia had no idea how to respond to this extraordinary request.

Possibly the boy understood this, for he smiled at her again.

"It doesn't matter if you can't do that. Momo is keeping records, and we're going to be careful. I'm not related to anyone at all, but some of us have brothers and sisters."

He paused long enough for Cornelia to ask a question. "Do you have *anyone*, Edsen?"

She saw his face change as he took in what she'd said. The smile wavered, and then firmed, and his chin came out. "I have Marianne. Well, she mightn't be mine, but I'm hers. Anyway, I'm glad I got to meet you at last. Now I have to go back to the lander with Doctor Suchet. Goodbye, and thank you for caring about us. Elydia out."

For a few seconds more she saw his intent face peering at her and then the screen went dark.

Woo puffed out her cheeks. "He wants *children*?"

"Orphans."

"Great God! That's positively mediaeval!"

Cornelia quite agreed. It was a preposterous idea. It would amount to an interstellar adoption service.

But . . . put like that it almost sounded possible.

Chapter Thirteen: Dorotea

Elydia 18 01 01
Doctor Dorotea Suchet

Dorotea had calculated she could spend twenty-four hours in her iso-suit before it became uncomfortable. Some people had stayed in them for days, but hers wasn't provisioned for that. She thought she could stretch the time for another twelve hours, or even twenty-four. She hoped so. It would give her time to distribute the information she'd brought, and to explain how to use it.

After Edsen's conversation with Cornelia Conti, she took him back to where she'd left the lander. Technically, it was a conglomerate vehicle made up of the lander *and* both shuttles. After a thorough examination of the damage, Terror Australis had said their chances of using the shuttles again came between Buckley's and none, and that keeping them aboard was not only useless but bloody irresponsible.

"They're infested, and it's gone and nixed the electronics," he'd finished.

Since they couldn't be moved under their own power, the choices came down to jettisoning them into space or somehow getting them down to the planet.

Spacing them would be easier, but irresponsible. What if someone in the future thought a crew was in distress and tried to rescue or salvage the shuttles? The only sensible thing to do was to get them down to the surface of Elydia. Luckily the lander, although its land-legs were compromised, could still fly. It was linked to the larger shuttles and provided the motive power for all three. The only difficulty with that idea was that the ungainly linked-up crafts would probably crash, and someone had to fly them. In theory, the lander could fly itself. In this case, it needed human judgement to try to hold the trajectory.

"It's suicide," the captain said in a flat tone when the idea was floated.

"It is," Harry Fejoa agreed.

"If it's not done, we'll all die," Dorotea pointed out. She went over the logistics of landing on either Terra or Shiva with three compromised vehicles and a human body full of a lethal substance.

They couldn't do it, even if it was allowed.

Indira herself was clear — so far. She'd never landed on the planet. If the shuttles, the lander and their cradles were all ejected, along with Ambassador Singh's body, before the silvering infiltrated *Indira* herself, all should be well.

"In any case, you can stay in space for a week afterwards," Dorotea said.

"What good will that do?"

"If the silver substance has got a hold on us or the ship, a week will be enough to tell," Doctor Benz said coolly.

Harry concurred. "If none of us dies of the racking, and if *Indira* doesn't glitch or crash or fall apart, we should be safe."

There was a good deal more argument, but it was the only way. As for who was going to pilot the conglomeration, that was never in doubt. Dorotea was older than any of them, except for Harry Fejoa. She had no dependents and no family. She had made a promise to the children of *Elysian Dawn*, and she was determined to see it through.

The crew and passengers of *Indira* were sad to see her go, but she knew they were also relieved. Trading one older person for dozens of younger ones wasn't a bad deal.

"You'll let us know when you've landed, and how you get on?" Daffodil Lan faltered.

Dorotea smiled. "No. I'll have a lot to do and not much time to do it. Don't worry, Daff. It will be all right."

"But what about the—the—"

"I won't die of the racking. I won't even have to suffer. We've been over that before, if you remember? Now cheer up, Daff. Go on home and have a good life. Put all this behind you." She laughed, leaned forward to hug the younger woman, and whispered, "And *don't* fall in love with Harry Fejoa. Find someone without a lot of baggage, or—oh, look at me! You do what you need to do to be who you need to be to do it. I always did that, and I'm still doing it now."

That was the last thing she said to anyone on *Indira*. She evaded a mass farewell by locking herself in the lander with the stasi-sheeted body of Ambassador Singh and turning off the interior communications.

There was considerable rocking and dragging to get the linked shuttles detached in their cradles, but then it was done, and she was away.

Of course, the conglomerate crashed.

Still, Dorotea told herself, any landing from which one walked away was a good one! And she walked away. She'd landed off course, but that was better than squashing any of the Elydians. And she was lucky enough to come upon Edsen Balm, who had seen her fiery re-entry and come to investigate.

Elydia 20-24 01 01
Doctor Dorotea Suchet

Dorotea squeezed six days out of her time on Elydia. She made careful use of the caffeine tablets she'd brought, to stay awake as much as possible. She found, to her pleasure, that there was no need to organise things for the ship-born. They were a capable bunch, and they made their own arrangements.

After she delivered the printouts and explained how to read and store them, she showed them the *peel-the-pear* map, and another of the Celestial neighbourhood. Edsen Balm pounced on that. "Oh, thanks! I've been trying to remember it! The ones we found at the Terra-tat were so basic."

They were thirsty for knowledge. They didn't want history, and they didn't want to know about Terra. They wanted to know the practical things their lost *Keepers* and *Heirs* would have known. They wanted, as far as possible, to live the life Outward-Bound had intended for their descendants.

"We're going to write it all down, so we never lose it again," Momo Moon told her. Momo was a sweet and serious person, and she was dedicated to learning anything she could about keeping the community healthy. She informed Dorotea she intended to teach everything she knew to as many people as she could, so there would always be Elysian healers.

"You'll be a sisterhood," Dorotea said, before reflecting that probably some of them would be men. She was unsure how the Elysians managed gender roles, as she saw as many of the male *Elves,* as the older ones called them, caring for little ones as the females did. Ages seemed fluid, too. Children who looked as if they should be dependent were managing themselves unfettered by their elders.

She thought regretfully of Claire, Finn, and Farne, and the four babies who'd died during the intervention. Would they have been happily integrated if *Indira* hadn't come to their rescue? And would little Amrita remember, as she grew to young womanhood and beyond, the man she'd known as *Meel*?

We meant well.

Since large groups including a disproportionate number of toddlers, ducks, and young goats were noisy, the older Elydians presented themselves in clutches of six or so, listened, recorded, and then asked questions. Dorotea had never considered her knowledge encyclopaedic, but she found she knew far more than she'd thought. The problem lay in presenting facts that built on what they knew already, and what they were in a position to implement. They had the stores in the hold, but they didn't know what some of them were, let alone how to use them. Dorotea identified and explained whatever she could.

"If you make fires for cooking, you can cut down on the wood you use by banking them down with damp turf. Do you have matches?"

They assented. "And flints," Granton said. He went to fetch some.

"I don't know if there is a source of wax or oil here, but if so, you might be able to make candles by melting it and dipping fibre in it. Do you know what tallow is?"

They didn't. Neither had they heard of bees.

"If an animal dies, there will be hard yellow fat inside. You can render that for fuel. Do you know what rendering is?"

Momo did.

"Do you have knives? You can use those to take the skin off dead animals. You might want to cook the flesh to eat. It has to be stored somewhere cool and used quickly. With the sheep, you can use shears to cut off the fleece without hurting the sheep." She described shears, as best she could, and Bede Arcadia went off to search the hold, returning with not only shears, but a spindle. "There's something else with them," he said, and described what could only be a large loom.

She explained how to make felt, and the very basics of

spinning and weaving.

"The trees you call woolwood might make cloth if you soak them in water and pound them."

They knew about flax, linen and hemp for cloth, so this made sense to them.

On and on, it went, question and answer. Now and then Momo or her sister Sakura would shoo everyone away so Dorotea could rest.

Marianne Arcadia, Edsen Balm, Sherry Cliffside, Hillman Hope, Granton Farsee, Zeb Carpenter, Momo Moon, a younger child named Tamma Windward and an even younger one named Bede Arcadia, brother of Marianne, seemed to be taking shifts, ensuring one of them was with her most of the time. She noted an imbalance of sexes at the upper end. At seventeen, Marianne was older than any others, and it seemed she and Sherry and Claire, who had died on *Indira,* had been the eldest female survivors.

Of course. Girls matured a little sooner than boys. And it seemed maturity was the key. Dorotea pondered probable causes. Was the presence of HGH what allowed growing children to live while others died? Or was it something to do with the age at which bone growth slowed? Some other hormone, perhaps? It would be a fascinating study, but she was here to increase their knowledge, not hers. This was something they would *not* have to know since none of them would ever leave the planet and no one could ever arrive . . . unless they were children.

Edsen had asked Cornelia Conti to send them children. That was something that might interest Daffodil. She had been part of a mass-orphaning on Terra.

She would not contact Daffodil. She must trust others to do what could be done in the future.

For her, there was only the present and not too much of that.

She stretched her time in the iso-suit to forty hours and then removed it.

The children stared at her, and she wondered why, before realising that of course, apart from Edsen's brief conversation with Outward-Bound, and the repatriated toddlers who'd spent a brief time on *Indira,* none of them had ever seen anyone even approaching her age. She was glad to recognise Amrita Kavya, Dashiel Shakespeare, and other little children she knew, apparently none the worse for their near miss — or for their vaccinations.

She should tell Daffodil that.

No. All her telling now was for the Elydians.

It was so good to be out in the air again. After her years on Shiva, she had almost forgotten the caress of the wind, the smell of sunshine after rain, and being able to look up into a gently cloudy sky.

She ate fruit and things they said were mushrooms and drank water from pondcups. She agreed some white tubers Tamma and her friend Aleph, another brother of Marianne's, had found, were safe to eat.

She suggested fences to keep goats, sheep and horses out of the gardens when they were planted and explained what saddles and bridles looked like, and how horses might be trained to accept them.

She was introduced to some little, quilted creatures that moved like mice. "Hey-muss," Edsen said, as pleased as if he'd invented them. He held down a piece of mushroom, and one of the bolder creatures swarmed up his legs to get it.

The look on his face was of pure delight.

"Heymice?" she questioned.

"Heymice. Yes. This is a heymice."

"Maybe heymouse, for just one of them."

He grinned at Marianne Arcadia. "There, Mim! I get to name things, too, with a bit of help from Doctor Dora."

Marianne gave him a one-armed hug and ruffled his hair in congratulation. They were affectionate friends, these two. In fact, they all were. Dorotea thanked her lucky stars for that. The little children would not grow up unloved. Already she saw them clumping into families-of-convenience.

One night, as she lay back on the soft grey-green grass, she had a feeling of déjà vu.

Suddenly, she was back farewelling Daffodil, and then back again, learning the peculiarities that were Shiva. She'd meant to stay there for five years, but somehow, she'd signed up for Shivan years instead of standard ones. Too bad . . . but more fool her.

Who did those Provosts think they were fooling, and what were they trying to do with their little Citizens?

She felt strange.

Back in the present, she still felt the oddness, as if time was behaving like a concertina.

"Can you sing?" she asked, abruptly.

"Not so well, but I play the flute," Sherry said.

"Jeremiah used to joke about playing the lyre, but he couldn't really do it," Marianne said.

"Play for me?" Dorotea reached into her pouch and withdrew a syringe. It was loaded already.

Sherry went off into a shelter and emerged with a wooden flute, which she started to play. Dorotea didn't know the name of the tune, and she didn't ask. She liked it.

As it finished, she felt the trembling begin in her limbs. She drew a deep breath. "I'm going to have to leave you now. I can either walk away a bit first, or just stay here. Which would you find less distressing?"

They didn't misunderstand her.

"Just stay here with us," Marianne said.

"We'll look after you. We'll put you to rest with Ambassador Singh," Sherry said.

"That will be good. I liked him."

Dorotea gave herself the injection, not wanting to wait any longer. She lay down and felt the drug take effect. No wise last words came to her, so she said nothing else, but she was aware of hands holding hers, a toddler curled against her, and a kiss on the cheek.

Chapter Fourteen: Fair and Just

Private Room, Provosts' Hall. Shivan Year 6 Day 639
The Provosts

Thirty-six Provosts attended the official meeting in the private room of Provosts' Hall. It was only the second time in the brief history of Shiva that the whole mustering had come together. At that time, it had been decided it was too risky for them all to be absent from their usual haunts at once.

It took three standard hours for them to arrive, as they came at staggered intervals. Not even they knew one another's everyday identities, and any of them who suspected kept that quiet.

To reveal oneself as a Provost, or to try to reveal another, would lead to instant expulsion from Shiva, and a fine which, coupled with the savage departure tax, would cripple the guilty one financially and socially.

And so, they arrived, entering secret doorways, stepping into hidden antechambers, dressing quickly in all-encompassing masks and robes before they entered the hall. Even their shoes were coloured, in case habitual footwear gave them away.

As the last one, a Rose, slipped into the private room, there was an audible sigh from those who had been waiting longest. A stranger in a gold robe stood at a lectern, ready to act as facilitator. Judging by her voice, she was Junoese, which would make sense. It was certain that she had no idea of the identity of any of the Provosts, and she had no ties with Shiva.

It had taken time to acquire Gold. That was why this extraordinary meeting was taking place a full seventy standard days after the unlucky event that set the affair in motion. Most of the Provosts would have preferred to get it over with much sooner, but they had to have a facilitator.

Gold read aloud from a prepared script. One of the Provosts was a bonder, and he, or she, had intended to bond Gold to remember and to reveal nothing of this meeting. To try remembering under a bond meant some unpleasant consequence — probably migraine or psychosomatic pain. Not that revealing the meeting would do much harm. Everyone knew the Provosts had a hall and met there. Presumably, everyone suspected there were more than six of them.

In the event, Gold had not been bonded. Gold was, indeed, a High Lady who had been utterly confounded and offended at the idea that she'd ever reveal a word spoken under the rose.

The meeting was about to begin.

Private Room, Provosts' Hall. Shivan Year 6 Day 639
Kat Lund

Kat counted herself lucky to be the last to arrive. When she slipped into her rose-pink robe, she tried to leave Katrina Lund behind. She was successful most of the time.

Only now and then did she find herself stepping out of character, and mostly, she pulled herself up with a snap. She'd messed up badly on *Indira*, not only moving to help Doctor Lan with the convulsing child, but breaking character to assure Doctors Suchet and Fejoa that no Provost would sabotage the *Indira* mission.

Afterwards, she'd feared another Provost would report

her, but evidently, she'd been the only one among the volunteers to go down to the cursed planet.

Behave yourself, she said in her mind. *Be careful. Be Rose.*

One of the Roses, anyway. She saw five others and wondered which two of them had been with her on *Indira.*

There were six Limes, too, which meant a total of eleven people who might have something to report about her behaviour on that mission.

Katrina schooled herself not to tremble as Gold spoke.

"You are called together to consider the ramifications of the rescue attempt made using the ferryship *Indira.*

"The primary public brief was to rescue Terrans from a planet where their ship crashed and to bring them to serve Mother Shiva.

"The secondary brief, not public, was to investigate the planet for its usefulness to Mother Shiva.

"The tertiary brief, not public, was to garner honour for Mother Shiva.

"The quaternary brief, not public, was to test the success of the Citizen project.

"Rewards sought included valuable assets, high esteem, Terran obligation, potential parents for Citizens and a benchmark in the Citizen project. A further offered reward was absolute ownership of the Terran company Outward-Bound."

Gold turned a masked head from side to side, as if reading their reactions. It must be a habit since the Provosts' faces were covered and their body-language carefully schooled.

"Is this a fair and accurate rendering of the affair?" Gold said.

Heads bent, and right hands lifted in acknowledgement.

Statistically, at least some of the Provosts *had* to be left-handed. Kat was herself. The original Rose was right-handed, so Kat lifted her right hand.

"Let us now examine the extent to which these briefs, purposes and goals were successful," Gold continued.

"The primary public brief was a failure, leading not only to the death of seven ship-born, but also to the death of Cleaner Jameel Singh, a Terran resident of Mother Shiva, temporarily classed as an ambassador, and the presumed death of Doctor Dorotea Suchet, a Terran paediatrician, bound over to Mother Shiva.

"The secondary brief was a failure. The planet is of no use to Mother Shiva. Although it undoubtedly has salt and minerals, these are not accessible. The attempt led to the loss of metallurgist Passim Dee, an independent Terran contractor.

"The tertiary brief was a partial success. There is honour in gallant failure.

"The quaternary brief was a partial success, casting some light on the Citizen project.

"Rewards gained include a benchmark in the Citizen project, along with absolute ownership of the Terran company Outward-Bound.

"Other losses include two shuttles, one lander and at least five comm-sets."

Is this a fair and accurate rendering of the affair?"

Up went the right hands, including Kat's.

"Regarding the second reward, absolute ownership of the Terran company Outward-Bound, do you regard this as a fair recompense for the effort, loss and costs associated with the affair?"

Heads remained still, right hands to sides.

"Comments?"

One of the Blueberries lifted shoulders in a shrug. "The company is worth nothing."

"It's the *First Launch* company, giving it great significance," a Lemon countered.

"It's worth nothing," a Tangerine reiterated.

"We could sue for costs." That was a Rose.

Behave yourself, Kat thought, but she couldn't help saying, "Didn't we get what was offered? A solvent company and all its assets? If you are promised a living animal, a mouse fits that definition as well as a pedigreed dog."

Gold said nothing. Evidently, this response wasn't covered in the prompts.

"Technically, we did get what was offered. In spirit and in fact, we were duped," a Lilac said.

"And whose fault is that?" Kat muttered.

A Blueberry gestured to Gold, who continued.

"This brings us to the second reward, the benchmark for the Citizen project. Comments?"

"Citizen Meera Singh made the call and the arrangements," the Blueberry said.

"Under whose guidance?" a Rose asked.

"Lemon, Lime and Blueberry were on duty," a different Blueberry admitted.

"Was any cautionary guidance offered to Citizen Singh?"

One of the Lemons stepped forward. "We thought it a good test case for Citizen Singh, as it would give her a chance to use her assets to evaluate the risk and possible rewards and to act with confidence. Had she refused, or hesitated to accept the responsibility, it would have proved she had no confidence in her judgement."

"Obviously, she did have confidence."

The Lemon concurred. "Feed from her *shindi* indicated determination and a degree of nervous excitement as well as pride and exultation."

"Unfortunately, confidence and pride were both misplaced," a Lilac said.

"It might have worked," Kat said. She was appalled to hear her own voice, but it was too late to take it back.

"Even if it had, it would have encouraged Terra to believe

it can depend on Mother Shiva to correct its errors. That is a bad precedent to set."

"Any way you want to view the affair, it shows a serious and unacceptable lack of judgement on the part of Citizen Singh, and on the part of three facets of Blueberry, Lemon and Lime," Tangerine said.

There was silence for a while, and then three Provosts in those colours bowed to the company and quietly removed their robes and veils. Faces set, the two women and one man stood revealed as their everyday selves for several seconds before they turned and filed out, leaving their robes behind them.

"Shoes," Tangerine said.

No one made a move, so Kat turned and followed. She didn't know what would happen to the disgraced three, but she did know letting them go out with their colour-coded shoes was a bad idea.

She caught up with them and passed on the request. One of the women flushed an unbecoming shade of puce as she fumbled to remove her blue-purple shoes.

"I'm sorry," Kat murmured, gathering them up. She wanted to give more sympathy, but she knew the real name of the one who had been Lemon. To let that knowledge slip would disgrace her as well. She bobbed her head and returned to the private room where she dumped the shoes on the discarded clothing.

"Need we discontinue Blueberry, Lemon and Lime?" Lilac asked the assembly.

"To do that would place an unacceptable burden on Rose, Lilac and Tangerine," a Lemon said.

"Better to find three more facets," a Rose said brusquely.

Lilac said, "Citizen Meera Singh has made a catastrophic error in judgement. This is troubling, as she has been one of our shining examples. Should we move to discipline her?"

For what, exactly? Kat bit down hard on her lower lip to avoid voicing that comment aloud.

A Blueberry said, "She has lost confidence and pride. She won't make such an error again."

"She must never be in the position to make such an error again," a Rose snapped.

"She has lost her brother, Cleaner Jameel Singh," another Rose put in.

Lilac said, musingly, "He was her only sibling? Terra-born?"

A Rose came to attention. "He was. I remember him as a child. He held her when I affixed the *shindi*. His mother was all pride and happiness because she'd won the *Ganges* lottery and come to Mother Shiva for the sake of a second child."

"Then she now has just one child, Citizen Meera Singh?"

"That's right," the Rose said.

This must be the original Rose Provost, Kat thought. If she affixed the *shindi* to one of the first Citizens, she must have been in robes for close to six Shivan years.

"I believe we have our solution," Lilac said.

Kat frowned behind her veil. If Lilac was thinking what she suspected, he was thinking . . .

"I move that Meera Singh and her parents be encouraged to repatriate to Terra. They will feel more comfortable there, and with a single child, Dev and Diya Singh won't be penalised by the Terran tax system."

Styx! They're going to throw her out for one error of judgement?

To be fair, it was a big one. *Indira* was back in service, but it had been forced to wait for its lander and shuttles to be replaced. The crew had been paid off, never to work for Mother Shiva again, and the three remaining medics had been informed that any application they might make for future employment would be regretfully declined. Then there was the problem of replacing Doctor Dorotea Suchet, who had not returned to complete her tenure. Explaining she had died while in the service of Mother Shiva was impossible. Equally impossible was the idea of letting anyone believe she had willfully left service prematurely.

Lilac gestured to Gold, who came out of an apparent trance and said, "It has been moved that Citizen Meera Singh should be stripped of Citizenship and repatriated to Terra, along with her parents. Is this a fair and just reaction to her failure?"

Thirty-two right hands were raised as one. Kat, still struggling with the concept of summarily disenfranchising a girl whose seventeen years had been lived in privilege and encouragement, became aware of thirty-three veiled faces turned her way.

Disliking herself, she raised her right hand. She wasn't really agreeing. That would require the use of her true-dominant hand, which was her left.

"Then it is unanimous," Gold said.

Surely that was the end? But it wasn't. A Tangerine had another motion to raise.

"We are agreed that the Citizenship project is not working in the way we envisaged."

Heavy sighs sounded, accompanied by gloomy shakes of the heads.

"We had planned, and fully intended, to hand over the management and welfare of Mother Shiva to the Citizens when the first twelve came of age. The disappointing matter of Meera Singh suggests this handover schedule was over-ambitious. It is obviously inappropriate to put such heavy responsibility on young and untested shoulders. I, therefore, move that we reconsider our timeline, or rethink the whole idea."

"Do you mean we should terminate the Citizenship project?" the original Rose asked.

"Not at all! I remain absolutely committed to the Citizenship project. All I suggest is that we enter a watching brief and let the Citizens mature into their roles. Further selection may be necessary to reach optimum potential. Perhaps in another two generations, we may revisit the idea of handing over the management of Shivan affairs. Until then . . ." Tangerine let the words trail off and lifted his hands in mute surrender.

"Until then, I take it, the Provost system will remain indefinitely," the original Rose said drily.

"It would be very wrong of us to burden brilliant young minds with decisions they are not qualified to make," Tangerine said. He lifted a hand to Gold.

"It has been moved that the timeline for winding up the Provost system should be extended indefinitely, to such a time as it is deemed the Citizens of Shiva show sufficient maturity to manage the planet's affairs. Those in favour, please raise your right hand," Gold said.

Thirty-two right hands presumably rose. Veiled faces presumably turned to stare down the rebel Rose, but to no avail. Katrina Lund had quietly flung off her robes, shed her shoes and left the building.

She had no illusions that her departure would sway the vote or the decision, and no illusions that her action would benefit Meera Singh, her bereft parents, her sister-in-law-elect or anyone else.

Her only feelings were of regret and dismay that something that had promised diamonds should have turned out to be nothing but dust.

Chapter Fifteen: "I'm In."

Rachel Foundation, September 3rd, 2273
Doctor Daffodil Lan

"I'm not welcome on Shiva anymore, Daff." Harry Fejoa didn't sound too distressed. If anything, he sounded pleased.

"I got served a keep-away notice, too," Daffodil admitted.

"But that's not why you came to see me?"

"No. I came to use you as a sounding board."

Fejoa laughed. "I've been used as a lot of things in my time, my child, but this is new."

"*My child*?" She raised her brows.

"Not literally. At least, not as far as I know. And I apologise for the implication. You're not a child, just a lot younger than I am. In theory, I could be your grandfather."

"Don't be scared, Harry. I'm not after your body, though I have heard canned fruit is just as nutritious as the fresh stuff."

He grinned at her. "That's good to know. I was going to contact you this week, but you pre-empted me."

"Really? What about?"

"That can wait. What idea do you want to bounce off me?"

"If I were to take up tanking, the way you do it, would it be possible to arrange for a wake-up call when certain conditions are met?"

He looked at her for a few moments, brows creased. "It's

possible, Daff, but tanking isn't a good idea for most people. It suits me, and in fact, I thrive on it, but you're untested. If you enter a tank, there's a fair chance you won't wake up."

"That's what happened to your wife, isn't it?"

"Rachel is my fiancée. We never got as far as the wedding."

"And she died in the tank."

"That's the official story, but Rachel's not dead. She's just comatose. As you obviously know, she's the second five-year tanker . . . the one who failed to rouse. What you probably didn't know is that I had her put back in a tank — my own system — three months after the unsuccessful extraction. There she stays until I, or someone else, works out a way to restore her. You have heard of cure-coasting, of course?"

Daffodil assented.

"So, Rach is cure-coasting. I spend a lot of time in the tank, too, so I won't be too old when she wakes."

"Too old for what? To marry her?"

"That, of course, but mainly, I can't risk being too old to be a proper hands-on father for our child." He chuckled at her expression. "You didn't expect that, did you, Daff? Rachel is tanking for two. We didn't know she was pregnant when we signed up for the fiver, but it showed up when they were scanning her after the non-waking event. That's how I got them to let me tank her again. Rach had signed a waiver, but our baby certainly did not. I caught them in a legal precedent. They tried the *unviable embryo* clause on me, but I played the *date of conception* one on them. By their reasoning, our baby couldn't possibly be viable and so was legally not a person. By mine, it should be school-age. It had been naturally conceived over five years before, had never been frozen, and so most definitely *was* a person." He held up his hand when she opened her mouth to protest. "I know, that's specious reasoning, but think of the headlines if they'd forced the issue!"

"So, whenever you go in the tank yourself, you leave instructions to be woken if there's a breakthrough in coma reversal?" Daffodil saw parallels with her own idea.

"That's about it. It's not instructions, per se. It's a key-word alert. If certain key-words occur in medical newsfeeds with the right frequency . . . it's an algorithm I worked out. I also have spies. But that's my situation and my choice. Also, as I told you on *Indira*, I would have been willing to throw in my lot with the *First Launchers* for a while if it had been possible. What about you? What are you hoping to wake for?"

Daffodil stared at his handsome face. He looked kind and normal. He sounded flippant and borderline fanatical. He was undoubtedly wealthy and ruthless. "I've been talking to Cornelia Conti," she explained.

"Outward-Bound. Nice woman. Did the best she could in a bad situation. She's on my list for this week as well."

"I thought—"

"You thought I was vengefully pursuing Outward-Bound? Not at all. What happened to Rach is not their fault. Now that Chavez is dead, I have no axes to grind with what's left of that company."

"You didn't kill him, did you?" Daffodil asked, not quite joking.

"No. What were you and Cornelia discussing?"

"We've both been thinking along the same lines . . . we very much want to help the ship-born on Elydia, but the only thing they asked for is more people to give them a viable gene pool. It's not crucial yet, and won't be for maybe three or four or more generations, but—"

"Where do you expect to find these people?" Harry asked. At least he wasn't turning her away without a hearing. "I don't see many folks wanting to move to a place that transforms what it doesn't kill. It would do no good, anyway . . . unless you're suggesting embryo transplanting or IVF for the girls?"

"Nothing like that. I can't see technicians wanting to risk landing there . . . not when there's a chance their shuttle won't take off again. Cornelia and I were thinking of sending them the orphans Edsen asked for."

Harry raised an eyebrow, which seemed to be a trick of his.

"I was orphaned in the great disaster of twenty-two fifty-eight. Remember that?"

He nodded without surprise. Obviously, he knew.

"There were a hundred-and-forty-three of us with no close relatives, and we must have put a terrible strain on the foster system. We weren't treated badly, and the insurance gave us a good education and every possible chance. It put me through medical training, and others were equally fortunate. Still, I think some of us would have been happy with a fresh start in a new community where we'd have been of value rather than a problem."

"Even a community where tech won't work, you have to do everything by hand, and you can never leave?"

"Even so."

"Your plan could turn out very badly. Kids who are inconvenient, ill, uncontrollable or unstable could be dumped there and forgotten. You'd be accused of sending them into slavery, or to their deaths. Parents or guardians might try to change their minds."

"We know. We were trying to work around that. Cornelia said Edsen suggested children of an age who would be at practically zero risk of the racking."

"We lost four small children and a pre-pubescent boy on *Indira*, as well as the teenagers."

"That was the result of their being removed from the planet. According to Momo Moon, no one younger than nine had even a twinge. Her family is a case in point. Both parents died, she, at thirteen, was in considerable distress, Sakura at ten had minor joint pain and Panji, who is seven, was unaffected."

Harry said, "It seems fairly safe then. But the logistics are difficult."

"As difficult as spending years in a tank, keeping your fiancée and unborn child in one for decades, while simultaneously finding time to train, work, travel and run a network of spies? How do you *do* that?"

He didn't answer directly, merely saying, "I take your point. But how does this equate with your own request to be tanked?"

"As I said, the need for new genes on Elydia won't be pressing for a century or so. And who knows, in a century or so, we might learn more about the silver substance, or develop a shuttle that it won't infiltrate. But I don't want to delegate the negotiations on this any more than you want to leave Rachel and your baby's welfare to strangers." She took a deep breath. "Cornelia and I thought we could do the initial research now, get permissions in place, and then tank ourselves to wake when, and if, there is a sudden influx of suitable children whose chance of a decent home is otherwise low."

"*Suitable* children?"

"Genetically healthy . . . screened as the *First Launch* people were. Of course, that goes against the Great Inclusiveness, but in this case, I think it's justified."

"Hmph. One problem is that only a legal adult can make an informed decision about the risks, but legal adults are the ones that have a hundred percent chance of dying. As you say, the younger, the safer, but also, the younger they are, the less likely they are to understand the implications of saying *yes.*"

"The alternative is to let the Elydian community die out or suffer genetic defects in future."

"Would they, though? They're pretty well screened for bad recessives."

"They might be all right," she allowed.

"And supposing you did send them a genetic care parcel, would those second-landers become an underclass? They might find themselves classed as breeding stock."

"I don't know, Harry. You're the psych expert. Would they?"

"I'm the man who spends most of his life in a tank."

"You won't help us, then?"

"I didn't say that." He smiled at her, looking sane and friendly. "It's a mad idea, Daff. But maybe we can consult with Gerd Benz and see what he says."

"He's a cold fish."

"He's a clever cold fish, and he met the ship-born. He even autopsied two of them. So, we could consult him, and Dov Talman . . . and wasn't there an unusually helpful Provost aboard? What do you say to getting all the volunteers from *Indira* together on this?"

"It could work?"

"Probably not, but dammit, I hate being defeated. So did Dorotea. She died to give the Elydians what she'd promised. We can serve them best by staying alive." He grinned at her, and added, "I have an admission to make . . ." He pulled out a comm-set.

"Are you supposed to have that? It's Shivan tech. Isn't it embargoed?"

"No, and not exactly, and yes, it is. But I know people who are quite good at retro-engineering and . . . let's just say I have useful contacts. Any interesting new tech finds its way to the Rachel Foundation. Just as well, since I was able to have one of these taken to Outward-Bound while I was still on *Indira*."

"How in—"

"Never mind. You probably don't want to know. Now, look." He touched the screen, and faces appeared, scrolling past, each animating and speaking a few words before giving way to the next.

A man with reddish hair stared out of the screen. "Commtech Dov Talman, ex *Indira*. I'm unauthorised, and I'm in."

A plain fortyish woman came next. "Katrina Lund, formerly Rose Provost, ex *Indira*. I'm angry, and I'm in."

"Gerd Benz. Surgeon. I'm in."

A very young woman stared solemnly out, said, "Harley Neel, Terra-born messenger on Shiva. I'm in." An impish smile spread over her face, and she lifted a finger to her lips and said, "Ssh!"

More and more faces animated and declared themselves. Daffodil recognised some, but most of them were strangers. A pretty Asian woman smiled and said, "Tanvi Kumar. In loving memory of Jameel Singh, I'm in." She turned and stretched out a hand, drawing a second woman into the picture, a beautiful girl with a scar on her forehead.

"Meera Singh. In memory of Jameel, my brother. I'm in."

A turn to the left and a handsome Asian youth with a scarred cheek smiled at them. "Ram Chatterjee, ex-Citizen of Shiva, now the terror of Terra. I'm in!"

A pause and then came a grumpy face that split into a disarming grin. "Speaking of terror . . . I'm Terrence *Terror* Australis, and I'm bloody well in as well."

Daffodil lifted wet eyes to gaze at Harry. "So many?"

"So many, Daff, and this is just the beginning. As I said, I was planning to call you in, but you pre-empted me. All of us feel the injustice of what happened as keenly as you and Cornelia. We're going to spend a while—not too long—

working out the logistics of this thing, and then we'll meet and set whatever we've decided in motion. Meanwhile, you and Cornelia can think about whether you really want to tank yourselves, or if you're content to leave that to the daft and the desperate, such as me. Deal?"

Daffodil thought of Dorotea Suchet's last words to her.

You do what you need to do to be who you need to be to do it. I always did that, and I'm still doing it now.

She put her hand in Harry's. "It's a deal."

Chapter Sixteen: Looking Forward.

Elydia 365 05.01
Marianne Arcadia

Marianne smiled up at Momo. "What do you think? Am I right?"

"You're always right, according to you." Edsen was twenty now. He was still solid, but taller than he had been. His hair, like Marianne's, was frosted with silver and his smile came more often and stayed longer.

"Quiet, sprat," she said.

"You can't call me a sprat anymore. Not now I'm a father!" He turned to Momo. "I am a father, right?"

"You're a father. Or you will be, in a while. I hope I remember how to catch and tie and all the rest."

Marianne said bracingly, "You were helping Moon deliver babies when you were eleven, Mo. You can do this. Anyway, you've been practising on sheep and goats."

"And horses," Momo said. She clicked her tongue. "Will someone chase those heymice away? They're heading for the mushrooms *again*."

Without looking round, Edsen roared, "Inga! Franz! Heymouse patrol!"

Giggling and chittering ensued.

Marianne got up from where she'd been lying on a fleece spread on the grass. She put one hand on her slightly curved stomach and held out the other to Edsen. "I wonder if it will be born silver?"

"The lambs aren't."

"Maybe it'll look the way we used to, then."

"Don't call it, *it,*" Edsen growled, putting a possessive hand on her waist.

"Okay. What shall we call—it? Carolina? Markus?"

"I don't think we should look back. Remember? New dreams now."

Marianne thought of Jeremiah Rain, whom she had loved so much when her only problem was gaining an extra centimetre in height.

She looked steadily at Edsen Balm, whom she loved in a different but no less fervent way. She couldn't quite remember when her affectionate gestures to a lonely friend became something she delighted in for her own sake as well as for his. It didn't matter. She was looking *forward.* "I think we'll come up with the perfect name when it—when the first new Elydian—is born."

"I think so, too." He put both arms around her with confidence. "I love you, Mim, but—"

"Now, Ed, *I love you,* can't come with a *but.* It just *is,* forever and ever," she said.

"I know that. I was going to say, *but have you got a mushroom in your pocket?*"

She laughed. "Um . . . yes. I get hungry. How did you guess?"

"It's easy to guess when there's a heymouse climbing up your leg."

The *Elydian Dawn* series continues in Book 4 *Rachel Outward-Bound*

Harry and his girlfriend, Rachel, planned a new life on the starship *Elysian Dawn* but fate and the Outward-Bound company had other ideas.

ABOUT THE AUTHOR

Sally Odgers is a Tasmanian wife and mother, grandmother, writer, reader, dog-lover, and tender of labyrinthine websites. She is fascinated by names and loves music and flowers.

Sally has been writing fantasy and science fiction for decades and loves creating new realities and series where characters wander in and out of one another's stories. One of her favourites is the *Fairy in the Bed* series which her alter ego Lark Westerly writes for eXtasy Books.

Sally and her husband are co-writers of a number of dog series for children. To find out more, visit the launching pad of Sally's website world at http://sallybyname.weebly.com